LETTERS
from
LEXINGTON

Lexington Main Street Association
103 W. China Street
P.O. Box 25
Lexington, MS 39095

LETTERS
from
LEXINGTON

by Phil Hardwick

Great American Publishers
www.GreatAmericanPublishers.com

Illustrations by Phil Hardwick
Cover art © Christine Balderas
Book design by Sheila Simmons

Other books in Phil Hardwick's Mississippi Mysteries Series:

1 • Found in Flora
2 • Captured in Canton
3 • Justice in Jackson
4 • Newcomer in New Albany
5 • Vengeance in Vicksburg
6 • Collision in Columbia
7 • Conspiracy in Corinth
8 • Cover-Up in Columbus
9 • Sixth Inning in Southaven

Great American Publishers
P. O. Box 1305 • Kosciusko, MS 39090
TOLL-FREE 1.866.625.9241 • info@gapublishers.com
www.GreatAmericanPublishers.com

For more information about the Mississippi Mysteries Series, visit the author's website at www.philhardwick.com

ACKNOWLEDGMENTS

The author acknowledges and thanks the following for their contributions to making this book possible:

The Lexington, Mississippi Main Street Board of Directors for their total support and assistance;

The many citizens of Lexington who told me their stories, allowed use of their facilities, provided background information or were otherwise instrumental in the project, including Don Barrett, Janice and Pat Barrett Jr., Jennifer Baughn, Ann and Charles Brown, Jacqueline Brown, Jean Strider Carson, Phil Cohen, Ann Fant Davis, Elder William Dean, Dayle Dillon Diffey, Antonio Durham, Dan Edwards, Brenda Farmer, Wirt and Lois Hayes, Saul Haymond, Bruce Hill, John "Kim" and Debbie Kimbrough III, Gwindolyn McRae King, Kristi Marshall, Elder James Rodgers, Billy and Sheila Russell, Jane and Holt Smith, Bonita Porter Spurlock, Darlene Ware, Chick Weathersby, and Darrell Williams;

Sheila Simmons, my editor and publisher, for past and present support and encouragement, and championing the Mississippi Mysteries Series.

Letters from Lexington *is a project of the*

Lexington Main Street Association

and was made possible by the generous support of...

BankPlus of Lexington
Peoples Drug Store
Russell's Drugs, Gifts & Collectibles

Janice & Pat Barrett Jr.

Dr. Martha Davis • Mallory Community Health Center
Porter & Sons' Funeral Home
Pro-Tech Ag • Agricultural Research & Consulting

Holmes County Board of Supervisors
Hunter Engineering of Durant, MS
Lexington Homes, Inc.
Lexington Concrete & Block Company
Mullen & Company CPA's

Holmes County Bank & Trust Company

Rick Dowdy • Holmes County Farm Bureau
Holmes County Chancery Clerk Jean Ford-Smith
Holmes County Circuit Clerk Earline Wright Hart
Hooker Insurance Agency
Bruce & Linda Patton MacMorran, Baton Rouge, LA
Riley's Bookkeeping Service
Twin Oaks Animal Clinic • Dr. Walter Roberts DVM
Wall Street Etc.

CHAPTER 1

Wednesday evening after prayer meeting, Ruthie Mae Hinds, wearing a summer print dress, stood under the light at the front door of St. Paul's Church of God in Christ in Lexington, Mississippi, and gave her friend Mildred Monroe a big hug and congratulations on her sixty-sixth birthday. Mildred wore her customary black pants and white blouse. Ruthie Mae's women's group at St. Paul's had given Mildred an affectionate birthday party even though Mildred attended another church just outside of town. Ruthie Mae and Mildred were the last ones to leave. They bid each other a good night and walked to their respective cars in the darkened parking lot beside the church.

It was the last night of October. Halloween. The evening was unusually warm for the time of year, making it comfortable for kids to be outside on an All Hallows Eve. The Halloween celebration this year had aroused a bit of controversy in Lexington. Several clergy members in town had called upon the city leaders to declare the Saturday before Halloween as the official "trick or treat" night, but the issue had been tabled after it was learned several churches were planning to have "fall festivals" on Wednesday evening after prayer meeting. The mayor was pleased with the thought that if this was the biggest issue in the month of October, then things must be all right in the little town of two thousand residents.

Ruthie Mae drove away with a wave as Mildred reached in her purse for the keys to her new Ford Mustang. She was Lexington's version of the little old lady from Pasadena if there ever was one. Suddenly she heard a swoosh from behind her as a bottle rocket and then a Roman candle erupted from the backyard of a house across the creek behind the church and spewed a trail of sparks skyward, followed by a pop and sparks falling from the blackness above. She looked up and stood watching as another shot from a Roman candle went upward. She heard children laughing. With a pleasant smile she unlocked the driver's door with the keyless remote device and pulled open the door. All of a sudden, she heard footsteps on the asphalt running toward her from out of the darkness.

Before she could react, he was on her. His body hit her with a force so hard, it knocked the breath out of her and slammed her against the inside of the front door. Her purse and planner/calendar landed on the front floorboard. The keys fell to the ground. She reached down to get the keys hoping she could hit the panic button which would sound the alarm on the car, but as she did so, his knee came up and slammed into her stomach. Shoved violently into the door once again, she had no way of knowing that internal bleeding had already begun. She attempted to scream, but no sound would come from her mouth. She dove into the car, hitting ribs on the steering wheel and landing on the front seat, her body halfway in and out of the vehicle. Her left hand reached feebly for her purse as pain racked her left side from broken ribs. Feeling the purse strap in her hand she clutched it tightly. She felt a hand grab her hair and then she was jerked backward out of the car by the attacker. Now too weak to resist, she slumped onto the asphalt. But he was not finished. Grabbing her by the front of her shirt, he picked her up as if she was a doll, spun around and pushed her up against the side of the car. Her assailant paused for two seconds and turned his head to a black Dodge Magnum sitting in the last parking space in the corner of the lot farthest away from the church building. His partner sat behind the wheel, watching and waiting. He looked back at the limp woman being held erect only by the force of his hand pushing her against the Mustang. His right hand went down into the pocket of his dark, baggy pants. Out came a Glock 17 9mm pistol which had been bought on the streets of Jackson a week before for only fifty dollars. He placed the end of the barrel on the center of her chest and fired one round—the sound lost in the myriad of fireworks. Mildred Monroe's body went limp and wilted to the asphalt parking lot.

He bent down, grabbed the woman's ankles and dragged the body twenty feet to a grassy area past the rear of the parking lot. He ran to the Magnum, opened the driver's door and said, "You drive the Mustang." The driver paused in confusion, but then exited the Magnum, raced across the parking lot, scooped up the keys and jumped in the Mustang. He cranked it, moved the transmission lever into drive and pushed hard on the gas pedal, making sure not to push hard enough to squeal the tires and draw attention. He did not know his left shoe had just transferred a small amount of the victim's blood from the paved surface to the carpet of the car. The Mustang lurched forward, traversed the parking lot, turned left on Highway 17 and accelerated away from the scene. The second vehicle waited momentarily and took a similar route, only at a much slower speed. Neither driver glanced back at the body of Mildred Monroe. If either had done so they would have seen a teenage boy and girl running to the victim and then dialing 9-1-1 on a cell phone. The call was answered immediately by the female dispatcher inside the Holmes County Sheriff's Department.

"Nine-one-one. What is your emergency?"

The breathless voice of a young man said, "Ms. Monroe has been shot and killed. Please send help!"

"Where are you, son?" said the dispatcher in a calm voice.

"St. Paul's Church. In the parking lot."

"Is the shooter still there?"

"No mam, he just drove away in Ms. Monroe's Mustang."

In a small town, most people really do know everybody else. And everybody who was anybody—no, even the people who weren't anybody—knew Mildred Monroe. The dispatcher knew Ms. Monroe and the car she drove.

"Which way is he heading?"

"Toward Interstate Fifty-Five, on Highway Seventeen."

"Stay right there. Help is on the way," the dispatcher said. She pulled the microphone to her lips and said, "Attention all units. We have a possible code seven in the parking lot at St. Paul's Church. Suspect just left the scene in a red Ford Mustang, heading southeast on Seventeen."

"S.O. three responding from downtown," she heard in her headset.

"Ten-four, S.O. three."

"S.O. one also responding,"

"Ten-four, S.O. one."

She looked across the radio console at the two men in uniform across from her. They were not law enforcement officers; they wore the uniform of an ambulance company. "We're en route," one of them said as they both leaped from their seats. Less than one minute had transpired from the time the call had come in.

"S.O. two," came the crackling transmission in her headset.

"Go ahead, S.O. two."

"I'm on Seventeen, about five miles out. I'll wait here to see if he comes by."

"Ten-four."

S.O. two, also known as Chief Deputy Roosevelt "Rosey" Adams, turned left off the highway and maneuvered his marked Crown Victoria police car to a narrow side road. He turned around and positioned it so he could quickly get back onto the main highway should the red Mustang come by. He did not have to wait long. The Mustang topped the hill to his left at approximately seventy miles per hour.

As the Mustang passed in front of him, Adams jammed his car's accelerator to the floor and steered the car onto the highway. Adams did not turn on the blue lights or the headlights, knowing the subject would merely speed-up even faster if he thought he was being pursued. As the Mustang went out of sight over a hill, Adams turned on the headlights. His vehicle's odometer quickly rose past fifty, then seventy and eighty. He topped the hill at eighty-five and saw red tail lights less than an eighth of a mile in front of him. His right foot began twitching; his breathing increased. These things never got routine. Both vehicles were heading southeast on Highway 17, and were less than two miles from Interstate 55. Adams was rapidly closing in on the Mustang. He deduced it must be slowing down. When he was thirty yards behind his quarry, Adams flipped the switches to turn on the blue lights and siren. As expected, the Mustang accelerated and started pulling away, the red tails lights appearing smaller.

Adams radioed in. "S.O. two in pursuit of suspect vehicle, southeast-bound on Seventeen, approaching Interstate Fifty-Five."

"Ten-four, S.O. two. Holmes S.O. and MHP being notified."

The Mustang braked hard as it approached the intersection, and then suddenly turned left into the parking lot of a well-lit convenience store and gas station. Adams slammed on his brakes and slid past the spot where the Mustang turned, but managed to also turn left into the parking lot. The Mustang sped around the back of the station, then the west side of the building and finally back onto Highway 17 and southeast-bound as he had been before. Adams' full-sized Crown Vic was not able to match the handling capabilities of the Mustang, and he lost ground on the subject. Adams figured the car had made a loop around the service station in order for the driver to throw drugs out the window, not an uncommon occurrence in pursuits nowadays. The Mustang crossed over the inter-state and continued southeast. Only a couple of miles ahead lay U.S. Highway 51—and a "T" intersection. Adams radioed in his new position as both vehicles screamed through the rural landscape past farmhouses and gravel side roads. A few of the houses had orange jack-o'-lanterns on their front porches. It took less than two minutes before they were approaching the intersection with U.S. Highway 51. Adams saw the welcome sight of a flickering blue glow in the darkness. Up ahead at the intersection were two sheriff's cars, blue lights flashing. The brake lights of the Mustang illuminated, its back end rose up and smoke billowed from screeching tires. The Mustang stopped so fast, Adams had to swerve off to the right shoulder of the road and lurch past the red car lest he rear-end it. Once back on pavement, Adams braked his vehicle, glancing in the rear view mirror as he did so to see the Mustang turning around and heading back in the opposite direction on Highway

17. As he made his U-turn, he saw the sheriff's cars heading his way. They blew past him as Adams completed his turn and rejoined the chase now heading back toward the interstate. Two minutes later, the Mustang crossed back over the interstate with three law enforcement vehicles in pursuit—their blue lights flashing and sirens wailing.

At that moment a traveler from Illinois who was gassing up at the service station looked up at the siren noise to see the Mustang skid past the left turn onto Interstate 55 South, then recover and swerve back toward the service station. The Mustang was coming directly at the gas pumps. At the last second the car slid sideways past the pumps, swerved again and somehow ended up back on the highway headed toward Lexington on the wrong side of the road. At that point, the driver of the Mustang saw the lights of an oncoming vehicle and swerved again, barely avoiding a head-on collision. The right wheels of the Mustang went off the road as the driver turned the steering wheel to the left. This action caused the car to turn sideways and begin a rollover across the highway, into a sign and chain link fence in front of a building known as The Little Red Schoolhouse. The doors flew open and were mangled as the car continued its flipping motion finally resting aside a large oak tree. Fortunately, for the driver, he was wearing his seat belt and shoulder harness and was not ejected from the vehicle. He appeared to have no sign of injury. But not so fortunate for the driver, he was immediately arrested, returned to Lexington, and charged with the murder of Mildred Monroe. His name was Rico Copiah and he was 17 years old.

CHAPTER 2

The Sunday after Thanksgiving, it rained steadily all morning. The weather reflected Jack Boulder's mood as he stared out the window panels of his balcony's French doors to the downtown-Jackson park two stories below. He loved this place, a condominium in the heart of downtown. He gazed to his left at the Governor's Mansion with its ten-foot white-brick-wall fence, knowing the first family had abandoned it last week for an eight-day trip to Paris. Boulder entertained the thought of chiding himself for not doing his normal five-mile jog this morning, but then thought better of it when a limb from an old sweet gum tree across the street cracked and fell to the ground with a thud. Where did that gust of wind come from? What the heck? It is cold and rainy, and a limb might have fallen on him if he had gone running. He might have even caught a cold. My, he could rationalize. Then the phone rang.

"Jack Boulder!" the voice on the telephone boomed. "This is Gus Rankin. How's my favorite private investigator?"

Rankin was a gregarious lawyer who had hired Boulder a few years ago to find out if his wife was cheating on him. She's a state representative from Gulfport who had to be in Jackson at the State Capitol during the legislative session. It was an easy case. The wife practically flaunted her affair with a north Mississippi state senator as they made the rounds of nightly legislative receptions and parties. She was in her late thirties; the senator was a happily married man of fifty-five with two grandchildren and a wife who was involved with seemingly every charity in their small town. Boulder had followed the couple around for six cold February nights in a row, and for six nights in a row, the couple attended an affair (pun intended) and then drove together to an apartment the senator rented three blocks from the Capitol. She stayed all night every night and emerged in the morning freshened up and wearing a different outfit. She was openly living there. Boulder sent a written report and sixty photos of the couple cavorting about town to his client Gus Rankin. The result was a clean divorce. Rankin confronted his wife with the evidence; she said she didn't want to be married anymore; there were no kids; and Rankin moved out. Rumors spread quickly in Gulfport about the sudden divorce, and Boulder, along with many news media, wondered aloud if Rankins now ex-wife could win reelection. She was in the second year of a four-year term, and voters forgave and forgot and elected her again. Boulder was informed that people on the Coast don't concern themselves with a politician's personal business, even if the politician represents them in the state legislature. On the other hand, the senator's constituents in north Mississippi did not forgive. The senator had an opponent who made "family values" the campaign issue resulting in the senator losing in the primary.

Subsequently, Rankin had called in Boulder to handle a variety of cases when there was detective work to be done in Jackson. None of the cases were very big or exciting. There was a workers-comp case where Boulder found the claimant, who had allegedly injured his back on the job, playing racquet-ball. Then there was a photo assignment of six lots in a new residential subdivision. Boulder never figured out that one, but he made a thousand dollars in less than half a day. Doing private-eye business with Gus Rankin had been easy and prof-itable. Perhaps he now had another such case.

"Hello, Gus," Boulder replied. "How's it going?"

"For me, it's going very well. Lost everything in the hurricane, so life got put in perspective for me. I moved back to my hometown of Lexington about a year ago. Got a little office on the south side of the Square. I decided to move from the fast lane to the slow lane and watch the traffic go around the county Courthouse instead of racing up and down the coast highway. Best move I ever made, my friend."

"Congratulations."

"I'm sorry to bother you on a Sunday morning, but I've got a client whose life is not so good. Someone he cared a lot about got murdered. He asked if I knew any good private investigators, and of course, you were the first to come to mind. Are you interested in taking on a new case?"

"For you, I'm always interested," Boulder said.

"He'll be arriving in Jackson tomorrow and will be staying at the Edison Walthall Hotel. His name is Grey Greene. Could you meet him in the lobby at three?"

"No problem. I'll get there a few minutes early, so tell him to just have the front desk page me. That name sounds familiar. Where's he from?"

"He's from Chicago. You may recognize him first. He's sort of well-known."

After a bit more small talk, Boulder hung up the telephone and walked across his living room. He picked up the remote control and aimed it at the flat-screen television sitting on a waist-high cabinet containing a hidden maze of wires connected to the various electronic devices. The cable company provided high-speed Internet access, cable television channels and telephone service in a package which is cheaper than buying such services separately. Boulder had planned to opt out of the phone service choosing to rely only on his cell phone, but it was actually cheaper to purchase all three services instead of only two. He switched the television to a news channel and then to another and then to another.

The newscasters were all talking politics, which meant there was no real news going on at this hour.

He walked over to a window and stared out at Smith Park, the square block of mostly green space across Congress Street from his condo. There was a small pavilion in the middle. On Sunday mornings it was filled with preachers using loudspeakers and attempting to save the souls of the homeless who showed up for a free meal. Boulder wondered who was fooling whom—the preachers who thought they may save a soul to guarantee their own salvation through good works, or the street people who would say anything for a free meal. The ritual was played out every Sunday morning, and Boulder played his part in the drama by sleeping until awakened by the loudspeakers.

Boulder pondered the scene and became philosophical. Why do people do the things they do? His thoughts turned back to the telephone call he had just received. Why does someone kill another person? No doubt he would find plenty of explanations.

He thought back to being in the police academy in St. Louis just over twenty years ago. In the class on abnormal psychology, the instructor had posed a question, "Is killing another human being a rational act or an irrational act?" The instructor allowed lively discussion and then pronounced, "A rational act is one guided by intelligence and reasoning, while an irrational act is guided by emotion without reason." More discussion and then Boulder himself asked the instructor, "But can't anybody rationalize anything? Killing another human being is rational in time of war or self defense, isn't it?" More good discussion and then the instructor said, "That's why they have juries."

He flipped the remote control to The Weather Channel, but found only advertising. He switched to a Chicago station. There was a professional-looking black man standing and talking about something. Then a name appeared at the bottom of the screen. Grey Greene. Boulder froze. It was Grey Greene, the same name as the man whom he was to meet tomorrow afternoon. He started to call his girlfriend, Laura Webster, and tell her, but he knew she was in preparation for a big trial tomorrow. If things went well he would see her at lunch.

CHAPTER 3

The Senior Judge of the United States District Court for the Southern District of Mississippi leaned back in the massive, black-leather chair and announced, "The noon hour has passed, the plaintiff has rested, and the jury is certainly in need of some nourishment. Ms. Webster, will you be ready after lunch?"

"Yes, your honor," said Laura Webster, attorney for the defendant.

"Court will be in recess until one-thirty," the judge said and then rapped his gavel softly in front of him.

The marshal shouted, "All rise," as the judge stood and departed the courtroom. After that, everyone else filed out. Laura Webster began collecting papers and stuffing them into her briefcase. One of the lawyers for the plaintiffs, a tall man in a dark-gray, pinstripe suit, approached her and said, "That was a very impressive cross-examination. That witness is one of the best experts in the country on the adverse effects of drugs. Would you entertain the idea of a settlement conference over lunch? Say...next door at the Edison Walthall restaurant?"

"Let me take care of some business and I'll meet you there in ten minutes."

The two lawyers who represented the plaintiff left the courtroom, one saying to the other as they walked out the door, "You told me she was good, but I didn't think she would be that good."

"You also didn't think she would look that good, did you?" he said with one raised eyebrow.

Laura Webster gave them time to get on the elevator then took the stairs down to the lobby where she found Jack Boulder, her lunch date, studying posters of the FBI's Ten Most Wanted. He was in his mid-forties and wearing khakis and a casual green jacket. She was the same age and had on a navy blue suit and a white blouse. She carried a twelve-pound briefcase full of papers in her left hand as though it was a file jacket. She glanced at the posters as she approached and then at him. "How's Mississippi's top private investigator today?" she asked with a grin.

"Couldn't be better," he replied. "The check from my most unreliable client cleared the bank, and the Camaro hasn't given me any trouble for awhile."

"You and that sixty-eight Camaro," she grinned. "At least the other woman in my life is a car."

It was true. Jack Boulder loved his fully restored Camaro too much. He bought it because of nostalgia, it being the first car he had ever owned, but he had seen a muscle car auction on ESPN a few weeks ago and learned the car had become a classic. Bidders were paying well over twenty grand for such cars. It would be silly to compare that "other woman" with Laura, his high school sweetheart and girlfriend for life.

Did Laura have another man in her life? He rejected the thought. If Laura Webster had another person in her life it would be the law. She was one of Mississippi's most prominent corporate lawyers. In the case before the court, she had shattered the testimony of every witness the lawyers of the alleged victim of a bad drug had produced. The plaintiff's lawyers in this case were a pair who rarely saw the inside of a courtroom. Their specialty was to find a drug mentioned as having some adverse side effects and then run television ads during the afternoon soaps soliciting clients who had taken the drug. Their strategy was to get the defendant drug companies to settle. But that would not happen in this case. The company had given Laura complete negotiating authority, and there was no way she would settle this case. She would even make a motion for a directed verdict when they returned to the courtroom.

"I'm sorry, but I'm going to have to cancel lunch. The other attorneys want to talk settlement over lunch."

"You must have destroyed their case."

"So what does your day look like?" she asked.

"I'll be over in Rankin County digging around early this afternoon. Then at three, I meet with a new client. You've seen him before. He's that crazy weather guy on the Chicago station on cable television. I'll tell you about it later. Good luck on your case."

CHAPTER 4

At precisely three o'clock in the afternoon, Jack Boulder's appointment arrived at the Edison Walthall Hotel in downtown Jackson, Mississippi. Gregory "Grey" Greene, the client from Chicago, stepped tentatively through the automatic, sliding-glass doors serving as a portal from the multi-story parking garage into the richly paneled reception area. Once inside, he assessed the long, narrow lobby running past the front desk, a seating area, a gift shop, a restaurant, and an open lounge to heavy, glass-paneled doors opening to Capitol Street. He raised his right hand to the designer sunglasses hiding his eyes and considered whether to remove them. Surely he would not be recognized here, seven hundred miles away from his usual abode. It was an occupational hazard for him. At first, he merely enjoyed the modicum of fame that blew down upon him like a breeze off Lake Michigan. It felt good to walk into any public place and have a complete stranger walk up and say, "I'm one of your biggest fans." Now he savored the notoriety. He had also come to enjoy the finer things in life that money and fame could bring. Suddenly, he felt haunted by the lesson of humbleness drilled into him by Ms. Monroe. He could hear her saying that fame and celebrity would be fleeting, and "...you Gregory Greene are no better or no worse than anything God ever created on this Earth." He wanted to be called Greg, but Ms. Monroe insisted all children under her tutelage be called by their given names. When he left Saints Academy, he began writing "Greg," but it came out as "Grey" because of the way he failed to enclose the loop at the top of the last letter. These days, people assumed the Grey Greene moniker was some type of television gimmick.

He took off the dark glasses, approached the wide front desk and was greeted by a smiling, handsome young clerk who said, "Checking in?"

"Gregory Greene. I have a reservation."

The clerk's face showed no sign of recognition. They went through the usual check-in procedure, after which Greene went to his room, dropped his overnighter on the bed, unzipped it, and retrieved a black-leather portfolio containing three letters. He returned to the front desk, had the clerk page Jack Boulder, and then stepped across the hall to the small gift shop about the same size as his master bedroom closet. He placed his right hand in the pocket of his black tropical wool, pleated trousers which had been tailored for him at a fine men's store in Chicago and walked slowly into the hotel gift shop. The pants went well with his cream-colored nine-hundred-dollar sweater and black Gucci loafers. The cut was perfect, for it made him look taller than his five-foot eight-inch height. He studied the magazine rack.

"Can I help you find something, sir?" asked the woman behind the cash register at the back of the room only ten feet away.

"Just browsing," he replied in an accent that sounded Californian to the cashier.

"Make yourself at home," she said.

"Do you have the *Chicago Tribune*?"

"Sorry," she replied. "We just have the *Wall Street Journal*, the *New York Times*, *USA Today* and the *Clarion-Ledger*. Or you can pick up the *Mississippi Business Journal* out there on the front desk counter. It's free for hotel guests." Without reply, he reached down, grabbed a *New York Times* and stepped to the counter. He laid the portfolio on the counter, placed the newspaper on top of it and reached in his pocket. "That will be a dollar," said the cashier.

"What about the tax?" he asked.

"There is no state sales tax on newspapers in Mississippi," she said with a grin. He handed her a dollar and a smirk. "How much tax do they charge in Chicago?"

His head popped up. "Who said I was from Chicago?"

"You're the television meteorologist, aren't you?"

His eyes locked onto hers. He did not ask, but if he had he would have discovered this woman behind the counter was only filling in for the cashier. Not only was she the marketing director for the hotel, she was also chairman of the hospitality committee of the regional convention and visitors bureau and she had a business degree from the University of Alabama. She also had a photographic mind and a memory that never failed. He paused and then turned his face slowly sideways.

"Do we know each other?"

She smiled and extended her hand. "I watch you on television when I go to Chicago." Instinctively, he shook her hand. She glanced down at their handshake, surprised his grip was so limp. "You're actually very good. And that article in *People* magazine last month said you were one of Chicago's most eligible bachelors. We're very proud of you. Went to school in Lexington, I believe. I have a cousin who grew up in Durant. Linda Starnes. She would be a few years younger than you. Anyway, you know how it is in Mississippi. We always want to know where you are from and who you know."

"I'm impressed," he replied. He studied her as he would the latest radar scan.

"No one would ever know you are from Mississippi. You've lost your accent, and you certainly don't dress like you're from the South. What are you doing in Jackson? You're not coming back here to be the new weather person on WLBT, are you?"

"I'm back in Mississippi on a personal matter. I'm supposed to meet someone here at the hotel."

"I promise not to tell anyone you're here," she grinned. "I know how you celebrities just cherish your privacy."

"For that, I thank you," he said as he turned around and made his way to a high-backed chair in the seating area of the hotel lobby. A few moments later, the front desk clerk walked toward him and said, "Excuse me. Are you Mr. Greene?"

"Yes."

"A Mr. Boulder called and said he would be a few moments late due to car trouble."

Greene stood and said firmly, "When he arrives, please tell Mr. Boulder I decided to get someone else." Greene turned and walked out the front hotel door.

At that minute, private investigator Jack Boulder was some four miles away, out on the shoulder of Interstate 20, staring at his fully-restored, but now mechanically-challenged, 1968 Camaro.

Coolant dripped from under the hood of his cherished automobile. Boulder looked back on the side of the road at the eight-foot-wide, greenish-yellow, liquid spot. Thirty minutes earlier he had been headed west-bound on Interstate 20 toward downtown Jackson after searching through land records at the Rankin County Courthouse in Brandon, a suburban county seat. As he passed the U.S. Highway 49 exit on his way back downtown, a red light on his dashboard announced trouble. While pulling over to the shoulder of the road, he had smelled engine coolant. He had immediately diagnosed the problem as a burst hose before the car had even stopped. He had called the front desk and asked the clerk to tell the man waiting for Mr. Boulder he would be late. He then called the Mississippi Highway Safety Patrol and requested the "nearest available" to be sent. That was police lingo for the dispatcher to call the nearest available wrecker service as opposed to one specified by the motorist.

Boulder recalled a homicide investigation he had conducted during his last year on the St. Louis, Missouri, Police Department. A virtual war had broken out among tow truck operators for business along the interstate highways around the Gateway City. A civilian police dispatcher was found beaten to death after his four-to midnight shift. Boulder discovered the dispatcher was involved in a scheme to steer business to a certain tow truck operator. When someone called and requested a tow truck, the dispatcher would call a certain company before calling the other tow truck operators. The dispatcher got greedy and wanted an increase in his cut or else he would tell the police. The tow truck owner responded by having his chief mechanic give the dispatcher a lesson using a tire tool. The mechanic got carried away and beat the dispatcher to a pulp. Boulder tied the dispatcher to the tow truck company by simply reviewing police calls the dispatcher had received and issued. It was a laborious process, but the scheme became obvious when studying the records. Boulder interviewed every one of the ten employees of the tow truck company separately, and it did not take long for the chief mechanic and the owner to start pointing fingers at each other. Boulder ended up with two convictions, one for murder and one for accessory before the fact. Towing vehicles was a lucrative business.

He saw a tow truck approaching, its yellow lights flashing. A white tow truck with a red winch growing from behind the cab whisked close by and came to a quick stop twenty-five yards in front of Boulder and his Camaro. Cars, trucks and eighteen-wheelers whizzed by noisily. The tow truck backed toward Boulder's Camaro as if reaching out to rescue the little car before it fell into the swift current of vehicles. There was a magnetic sign on the driver and passenger doors reading Jack's Towing Service. Boulder walked forward and greeted a pot-bellied man in his late twenties who wore a baseball cap with the number 24 on the front, blue jeans and a grease-stained tee-shirt promoting a certain brand of motor oil.

"That was fast," Boulder shouted above the traffic noise.

"You call. We come," said the man as he squatted down and peered under the front bumper of the car. "Don't see many rear-wheeled-drive cars much anymore. This one's a beauty. I'll take care with her. You can bet on that. Do you want me to take it to a certain garage or to our lot? All we do is towing. We don't do repairs."

Take it to Capital Automotive on State Street. They do all my mechanical work."

"Will do, sir."

The tow truck operator leaned on the side of his truck, pulled a lever, and the wench lowered in place. He worked fast, and in minutes the front end of the Camaro was raising upward, attached securely to the tow truck."

"Can I ride with you?" Boulder asked.

"Sorry, but regulations don't permit riders. I can have my dispatcher send a cab right out though."

"Yes. Please do. How much do I owe you?"

"Sixty dollars," the man replied in a matter-of-fact manner.

"Do you take cash?"

"Yes, sir. Cash is always welcome," he replied with a grin. Boulder pulled out a money clip, extracted three twenties and handed them to the man. The tow truck driver grinned and nodded his head forward in a mini-bow. Boulder noticed brown, tobacco-stained teeth.

At that moment, a white taxicab pulled up behind the two men. The driver was a darkly-tanned woman in her late twenties, perhaps early thirties.

"Need a ride?" she asked in a voice sounding like south Florida.

"I do," said Boulder as he climbed into the cab. "The Edison Walthall Hotel."

CHAPTER 5

Jack Boulder walked briskly to the front desk and said, "I'm Jack Boulder. I was supposed to meet someone..."

His sentence was interrupted by a change in expression on the desk clerk's face. It was a bewildered stare past Boulder. From behind him came a voice.

"He's right behind you."

Boulder turned, and there was the man on his television yesterday. Greene has, indeed, left the hotel after learning Boulder would be late for the appointment. He took a slow walk, quickly cooled off, and decided to come back and see what Boulder had to say. He heard Boulder ask for him just as he was coming into the hotel lobby. Grey Greene's left hand held a black-leather case. The right hand came out. "I'm Grey Greene."

"Good morning. I'm Jack Boulder. My apologies for being late, but my car broke down." Greene reacted with an understanding expression, but Boulder deduced that he did not believe a word of it. "Why don't we go to my office? It's right across the lobby." They took seats in a cozy area that looked like a study or library in a country estate. "So, how can I help you?" Boulder asked as he sat down in a large, winged-backed chair. Greene settled onto the large, stuffed sofa.

"I need someone to find out who sent a letter to me. Attorney Gus Rankin recommended you." Boulder nodded, and Greene continued. "The letter came to me the week before Thanksgiving and supposedly came from Ms. Monroe, but that would be impossible because she was killed on Halloween night." He reached in the black-leather case, produced a piece of paper, and handed it to Boulder. Stapled to the letter was an envelope with a Mildred Monroe return address and Gregory Greene's address in Chicago. The envelope was postmarked from zip code 39095—Lexington, Mississippi. The letter was typed. "Go ahead. Read it."

SOS
SAVE OUR SAINTS

Mrs. Barbara Calhoun
Mr. Gregory Greene
Miss Gwendolyn Warren
Rev. Robert Lauderdale
Mr. Gus Rankin

My Dear Friends:

I hope the Thanksgiving holidays find you well this year. As you may have heard, I am not available to personally follow up on this request with a telephone call because someone murdered me. It was not the random act it appeared to be. Those who say they cannot talk can talk.

Please consider continuing your contribution and remaining a member of the 50-K Club. You know how much it is needed and appreciated. With your help, Saints will come marching in again to Lexington.

From the other side,

Mildred Monroe

"Very intriguing," Boulder observed.

"Mildred Monroe was my senior English teacher in high school, which was Saints Academy in Lexington. It's been closed for a couple of years now. It's a private school owned by a church group. Ms. Monroe is—or should I say, was—trying to get it reopened. She's been teaching there forever. Man, that school was her life. Anyway, she got those five people at the top of the letter to contribute ten thousand dollars each year to help get the school reopened. For the past two years she has sent out a letter the week of Thanksgiving telling us how much she appreciated our past contributions and reminding us of the next year's contribution. This year we got this letter. It was certainly a surprise considering she died a month before"

"How was she killed?"

"Shot by a carjacker in a church parking lot," Greene said, shaking his head. "Man, that's hard to take."

"Anybody arrested?" Boulder asked.

"Some punk. I hope they put him under the jail."

"So what do you need a private investigator for?"

"Well, obviously, if she's dead, it wasn't she who sent this letter."

"So you want me to find out who sent the letter?"

"Yes."

"Do you know if the other people actually received this letter?"

"I know Gus Rankin did. He's as anxious as I am to find out who sent it."

Boulder thought it curious that Rankin had not said anything to him about the letter. "And the others?"

"I haven't talked to them."

"Do you know how to get in touch with them?" Greene leaned forward and motioned for Boulder to hand him the letter. He took and studied it.

"Ms. Calhoun is probably in the Jackson telephone book. Her husband was a huge supporter of the school and has more money than he could ever give away. Gwen Warren is still in Lexington. She's a doctor of some kind. We were in the same class. Reverend Lauderdale is the pastor of the church Ms. Monroe attended. I'm not sure what it's called, but it should be in the book under the preacher's name."

Boulder reached out and took back the letter. "Why do you think this letter was sent?"

"That's what I need you to find out."

"Any idea about who might have sent it?"

"Not a clue."

"Tell me about Mildred Monroe."

"She was a strict, but caring teacher. In her own way, she was really cool. She had a way of tearing you down and then building you back up if you know what I mean. She pushed me to do better all the time. She helped me get into college. Also told me I had a way with words. She really was a motivator."

"Was she married?"

"Not to a man. She was married to that school. That's all she cared about. When it closed, she was really mad. She went to see somebody at the church that owned it and was told it was strictly a financial decision. She said they told her the school lost too much money and they couldn't afford to keep it open. So she just informed them that if money was the problem, she could raise the money herself. Apparently, they told her they had to see it to believe it. She called some others and myself and asked if we would make a pledge to contribute ten thousand a year for five years. My understanding is the names on this letter are the ones who agreed to do that. She probably had some others who agreed to contribute a smaller amount. She called us the Fifty-K Club."

"This letter asks you to keep contributing," Boulder said. "To whom would you send the contributions?"

"She filed the papers to start a foundation—that SOS Save Our Saints on the top of the letter there."

"How often did you hear from her?"

"Just these letters for the past two years," Greene said. "I came down to a dinner in Lexington when she started the SOS thing. I guess there were about twenty people there, but these five made the big commitment."

"Okay. I'll look into it and call you if I find anything."

"Any idea how long it will be?" Greene asked.

"Give me a couple of weeks."

Greene handed Boulder an envelope, and said, "Here is your fee and my contact information. That should motivate you." Boulder opened it and discovered Greene's business card with a handwritten cell phone number on it along with a cashiers check payable to him in the amount of $10,000. "Is that sufficient? Attorney Rankin said you prefer to work on a flat-fee basis instead of by the hour."

That was true, thought Boulder. In his experience, clients who wanted an hourly rate, plus expenses tended to go into shock when the bill arrived. A flat fee eliminated that possibility even though it could carry more risk for Boulder. Although it did not happen very often, he had actually lost money on flat-fee cases. Sometimes simple cases turn into complicated cases. He folded the envelope and put it in his pocket.

"I'll call you when I have something," Boulder said.

They shook hands awkwardly. Boulder watched Greene walk across the lobby to the elevator. He wondered about this little man. He seemed haughty but uncomfortable. He did not warm up to this client, but the case was reasonably inspiring. That was something he had not had lately.

Boulder thought for a minute about the big check in his pocket. He rubbed the envelope with his thumb and fore-finger, and then realized there was something missing in his pocket—his car keys. Oh yeah, his car had broken down. He fished out the business card from his other pocket and dialed the number for Jack's Towing Service on his cell phone. The voice he heard was familiar to almost every American who has ever dialed a telephone number. "We're sorry. The number you have reached has been disconnected. If you feel you have reached this message in error, please hang up and try your call again." Boulder dialed the number on the card again. This time very carefully. Again, he got the same recording. He went to a phone booth across the lobby and looked in the business pages for a "Jack's Towing." No listing. He took a deep breath and dialed Deputy Chief Morgan Jones, his boyhood friend who now headed up the Operations section of the Jackson Police Department. He told Jones what happened.

"I've got bad news for you, Jack," Chief Jones said. "We've been trying to catch that gang for a month. It's the same M.O. every time. They find a motorist in distress and tow the vehicle away. Very conveniently, a taxi pulls up and takes the person to his destination. We know of a dozen cases so far, and we've got a task force working on it. Hold on a second." Boulder heard muffled voices on the telephone. "Sergeant Humphreys with the Highway Patrol is heading it up. He's here in my office right now. He wants to come interview you."

"Tell him I'll be in the restaurant at the Edison Walthall Hotel."

Chief Jones then took the description of Boulder's Camaro. Boulder walked back toward the Capitol Street entrance to the hotel. The restaurant was on his left; the bar was on his right. Fortunately, the bar was closed.

CHAPTER 6

Jack Boulder asked for a table for two and was seated at a small table by a window looking out onto Capitol Street. Thoughts of vengeance filled his mind. Whoever took his car was going to pay. It was not just any car either. He had spent thousands of dollars restoring it to almost original condition. Several times he had been offered twice what he had in it.

Only yesterday he had wondered if he was too obsessed with the car. He had a talk with his girlfriend Laura about it. She knew him like one of the mystery novels she was so fond of reading. He thought he knew her too, but he did not dwell on those thoughts. That's the difference between men and women, he concluded. Laura Webster, attorney at law, asked him a direct question like the trial lawyer that she was. "Do you like the car, or what it represents?" He knew the answer before the words came out of his mouth. His 1968 Camaro, with its 327 cubic-inch engine and four-speed transmission, represented youth. No, it was more than youth. It represented anticipation. Anticipation of life. He was in his mid-forties now. So was Laura. During their high school years, they rode around Jackson, Mississippi, in a new Camaro almost identical to the one that had just been stolen from him. He loved to ride out Robinson Road toward Shoney's Drive-In and let his right hand shift through the gears, then oh-so-subtly allow it to come to rest on the inside of her leg. She would respond by picking up his hand and holding it in hers. Ah, youth. Yes, that's what his 1968 Camaro represented. And now some scum of the earth had taken it from him. He decided when the toads were arrested, he would stick a sharpened number two pencil in their ears so they could never hear again. As he got lost in the thought of his retribution, he heard a voice say, "Jack Boulder?"

It was Sergeant Kenneth Humphreys of the Mississippi Highway Safety Patrol. He was a six-foot-tall, linebacker-built, state trooper with a buzz cut. He wore blue jeans, a dark blue tee-shirt, hiking boots and a tight-fitting, brown-leather coat. Boulder considered the look and figured Humphreys had been watching too much television. Besides, the impression of the gun was clearly visible on the lawman's hip.

"Hello, Sergeant," Boulder said as he stood up and extended his hand. "Good to see you."

Humphreys returned the handshake and said, "You the same Jack Boulder that wrote that book about how to get even?"

"I'm afraid so."

"That was a good thing you did," Humphreys said steadily. "I'd shoot somebody too if they killed my partner and his family." Humphreys was referring to Boulder's last days in St. Louis when Boulder's partner, and his partner's wife and child had been murdered during a house burglary. At the arraignment of the perpetrator, Boulder had shot and killed the man. Boulder was charged with murder by a politically motivated district attorney. During the trial, Boulder wrote down ways to get even with people who had wronged someone else. The book became a bestseller for a short few weeks, giving Boulder enough income to move back to his boyhood home of Jackson, Mississippi. The jury announced it was hopelessly deadlocked. The D.A. subsequently lost his bid for reelection and did not seek another indictment.

Humphreys slid into the chair across from Boulder, and they ordered two black coffees. The Highway Patrol investigator pulled out a small note pad from his jacket pocket and laid it on the table. Then came a cheap, ballpoint pen.

"Description of the vehicle?"

"Nineteen sixty-eight medium-blue Camaro. Stripe around the nose."

"Not many of those on the streets anymore," Sergeant Humphreys said.

"I know."

"Got a serial number or tag number?"

Boulder pulled out a black, hand-sized electronic organizer, referred to it and gave Humphreys the tag number and the vehicle identification number. Sergeant Humphreys informed Boulder that a lookout had already been given to law enforcement in central Mississippi after he had called earlier.

"I hate to give you bad news, but I think you may have been a victim of the Tow Truck Interstate Gang."

"The what?" Boulder asked.

"That's our name for them. They have stolen at least thirteen cars in the past fifteen days. The M.O. is the same as in your case. A tow truck pulls up to a motorist who has broken down on the side of an interstate highway. Sometimes the motorist has already called for a wrecker and just assumes his call is being answered."

"That's what happened to me."

"In other cases the tow truck pulls up as if by coincidence. Most drivers are so happy to see help arrive, they don't question the fact that they haven't called for one."

"A taxi showed up too," Boulder said.

"That's part of their operation. Just like the tow truck, the taxi just happens to be passing by."

"How many vehicles have you recovered?"

"There is where the really bad news comes in," Sergeant Humphreys said. "We haven't recovered even one. We think they have a warehouse somewhere in the area, but we don't have one solid lead other than a few descriptions. It looks like there are at least three men and one woman involved. Descriptions can be unreliable though. People have a tendency to forget."

"Or try to help the police with a description that may be inaccurate." Boulder then gave Humphreys the descriptions as he remembered them.

"This is consistent with some of the others," Sergeant Humphreys said.

"Let me give you my cell number. I'm going to be out of town the next few days." Boulder did so and they wrapped up their conversation. Humphreys promised to call him later with a case number for his insurance company. Boulder left the restaurant and began planning his investigation. He did not notice he was being followed.

CHAPTER 7

Boulder walked two blocks to his condominium overlooking Smith Park and went straight to the computer in his home office. The Internet had become an indispensable tool for finding information about people. Go to a certain website or search engine, type in an address and the name of the resident would magically appear. These days, typing in a telephone number on the right website could result in a name and address. He had been slow to adjust to computer technology, but now he relished it. It was not only a time-saver but as valuable an information-gathering tool as had ever been invented. He knew its possibilities and its limitations. For example, a photograph of someone on an Internet website was to be taken with the proverbial grain of salt. A teenager using photo-editing software could cut someone's head from one picture and paste it on someone else's body, and then place the new "person" in another environment, such as walking in a door or having dinner at a restaurant. Still, for basic information, the Internet was hard to beat. Even the card catalogues of many libraries could be found online.

He typed "Grey Greene" into the box on the screen of his favorite search engine. A dozen listings appeared. Half of them were related to Greene's position as meteorologist at his Chicago television station. He clicked on each and found little useful information. One website link was to a Chicago magazine article about the Windy City's most eligible bachelors. Greene was listed as such, and a profile was provided stating he lived in a condo on East Huron, drove a BMW and drank a certain brand of scotch. He preferred women who liked to party, and his idea of a good date was a ride on a Lear jet to New York for a Broadway show followed by dinner at Tavern on the Green in Central Park. There was no mention that he was from Mississippi.

The computer search for "Mildred Monroe" produced an online newspaper article about the murder. It did not give any new details but quoted Holmes County Sheriff's Department Chief Deputy Roosevelt Adams as saying, "It appears the victim was killed during an apparent carjacking."

Boulder printed out all the web pages and placed them into a file jacket. He used a black marker to write "Greene, Gregory" on the tab. He then telephoned a local car rental company and made arrangements to be picked up at 8:00 a.m. the following morning. He then called Laura Webster's administrative assistant at her law firm office and told her he was heading up to Lexington. His next call was to Chief Deputy Adams. After identifying himself and his purpose, he sought an appointment with the officer. Adams was only too willing to oblige.

"Tomorrow morning at ten would be a good time for me," Adams said.

CHAPTER 8

As promised, the rental-car company picked him up on time the next morning, and at 8:30 a.m., after signing the necessary papers, Jack Boulder settled into a silver Malibu that had just been returned by another customer. The interior had not been cleaned and it smelled that way. The windshield also looked in need of cleaning. He turned on the wipers and pushed in the windshield wash button. Small streams of water assaulted the windshield. Good, he thought. The wintry, gray sky promised rain. He would need the windshield wipers today. He started to go back inside and insist on a car that had been cleaned but time was of the essence.

Jack Boulder headed up Interstate 55 from Jackson to Lexington. Had he studied his rearview mirror, he would have noticed a maroon Mercury was maintaining a ten-car-length distance behind him.

Ten miles north of Jackson, Boulder's cell phone rang. It was Sergeant Humphreys of the special Highway Patrol task force investigating the tow truck theft gang. Humphreys wanted to give Boulder a case number for his insurance company. Boulder pulled over to the side of the road and wrote down the number. Humphreys told him there had been no further progress on the investigation. Boulder pulled back onto Interstate 55 and resumed his trip. Within a quarter mile he noticed a large, dark-red, four-door sedan emerge from an entrance ramp and maintain a position behind him. Was he being followed? Something did not feel right. He lowered his speed by ten miles per hour. The Mercury did the same and maintained its distance.

A few minutes later, Boulder took the next exit and drove east toward the town of Canton. The Mercury made the same turn and kept its distance. There was no doubt now in Boulder's mind, he was being tailed. Up ahead he saw a fast-food restaurant. He turned left and pulled into the drive-through lane. He watched his rear-view mirror, but lost the Mercury when he turned into the parking lot. He followed the lane to the rear of the restaurant and ordered a cup of black coffee. As he pulled around from behind the building and approached the checkout window, he spotted the Mercury sitting in the parking lot across the highway. He took his coffee and handed the cashier a dollar bill. While waiting for his change, he surveyed the landscape. Boulder pulled out of the restaurant driveway and took an immediate right into the parking lot of a convenience store. He got out and walked up to a public telephone near the front door. He dialed 9-1-1 and said, "The man who has been selling drugs at the high school is now parked in the lot across from the Quick-Stop convenience store on Highway Twenty-Two at Interstate Fifty-Five. He is driving a red Mercury. Be careful. He's got an automatic weapon in the car."

Boulder hung up the telephone and walked into the store. He went to the cooler and pretended to be deciding what to purchase while keeping one eye on the car across the street. After a couple of minutes he picked up a bottled water and took it to the teenage male cashier. As he was paying for it, he saw two marked police patrol cars and one unmarked police car converge on the red Mercury. A total of four officers jumped out with guns drawn.

"Man, would you look at that?!" said the cashier excitedly.

The driver's door on the Mercury slowly opened, and a man slid out with his hands in the air. He wore dark pants and a black and red letter jacket. Boulder guessed his age as late thirties. He looked a lot like a guy on television last night in one of those car advertisements where the guy screams at the camera.

Boulder got back in his car and drove across the street to get a better look. He did not recognize the man, concluding only that he was not the TV car salesman. The man looked at Boulder and gave him a cold stare that said, "I'm going to get you." The look told Boulder a lot about the man. An amateur would have pointed to Boulder and excitedly told the police to stop him. A professional would stand there silently, let the police do their checking and then move on. This was a professional.

Boulder drove to a spot far enough behind the Mercury to get the tag number. It was a Mississippi tag from Attala County, the county adjoining Holmes County to the east. He dictated the three digits and three letters into his cell phone recorder and then drove slowly away. In his side-view mirror he saw one of the uniformed police officers holding up a gun that had apparently been found inside the car. A smirk disguised as a smile crossed Boulder's lips. You want to play games; I can play games too.

He drove back out to Interstate 55 and continued north. As he did so, he began thinking about what had just happened. If his follower was related to the Gregory Greene case, then he probably knew Boulder was on the way to Lexington. If that was the case, a call could be made to someone ahead who could intercept him. He decided an alternate route might be a good idea instead of continuing straight up the interstate. He took an indirect route and arrived in Lexington shortly after 10:00 a.m. Chief Deputy Adams was waiting for him when he walked in the front door of the sheriff's department.

CHAPTER 9

When the name "Rosey" Adams was mentioned in Lexington, it was said with reverence. Roosevelt "Rosey" Adams was the pride and joy of Holmes County. He had played professional football and then returned to his hometown instead of going off to some glamorous-sounding place and building a mansion, forever forgetting where he came from. The "Rosey" nickname came from early school days when he was observed by several other boys when offering a red rose to a girl in his class with whom he had become smitten. He was in one of those classes where every student had a nickname. In his fourth grade class there were Shady, Skinny, Dopey, Wetsy, Rim, She-Girl and Pockets, just to name a few. He was smaller than the other children in the class and might have been nicknamed Runt, but that name had already been taken by Rodney Lincoln, a short, bony kid who stayed that way at least until graduation when he went away to some community college in Tennessee where his grandmother lived. Nobody in Lexington ever saw Runt again. Fourth grade was kind of tough for Rosey; he got picked on a lot due to his shyness. Then came fifth grade and puberty. In no time, Rosey shot up like a beanstalk and then started adding weight. By sixth grade he was a foot taller and forty pounds heavier than any other boy in class.

When high school football rolled around, he played linebacker on defense and tackle on offense. He was so good, colleges from all across the country came looking at the quiet young man with skin the color of dark chocolate and an ACT score of thirty. His house in Lexington was practically a tourist attraction as coaches from all over the country came to town to break bread with his mother and just get to know the family. His high school football coach loved to say Rosey never sacked a quarterback; he just scooped up the entire backfield and kept throwing away players until he found the one with the ball. He signed with Mississippi State and after a stellar college career, played with three professional teams before retiring at age thirty-four.

He then returned to Lexington where he became a sheriff's deputy, a job he had known he wanted since junior high school when a police officer befriended him after he was falsely accused of shoplifting a candy bar from a grocery store. The store manager thought Rosey had slipped a Milky Way into his pocket, so he made Rosey sit in a back room while he called the police. Rosey knew he was innocent, but he also knew he stood a good chance of going to jail or at the very least being taken home and indicted in front of his mother. The longer he sat in the folding metal chair against the wall in the back room, the more his fear caused his body to tremble. When the police officer came in the room, Rosey was so stressed that he was shaking and crying. The officer told the manager he would like to be alone with the juvenile for a few minutes. As the door closed, young Rosey looked at the officer's large, black belt and the attachments it held—a holstered pistol, hand-cuffs and extra ammunition. When he saw the handle end of a blackjack sticking out from the back pocket, Rosey pulled his knees to his chin and hugged the wall in the fetal position. The officer stood over him for a moment taking in the large, shivering teenager before him. He was a man with silver hair and lines on his neck and around his eyes. In a serious voice the police officer told him he would have one chance to tell the truth and "By the way, I already know the truth." The question was whether Rosey would tell the truth. Rosey knew that even if he told the truth he would not be believed, so he decided to confess to a petty crime he did not commit. He looked up, past the big silver badge and into the eyes of the police officer, and detected kindness, maybe even a hint of a smile like he saw in his grandfather's face. Yes, this man reminded him of his grandfather, a man he would never lie to. So he told the officer he did not steal the candy, but he thought it had dropped down between the racks. "Okay," the officer said. "I'll be right back." In a few minutes the officer returned with the store manager beside him. It was crowded in the back room. Rosey began to feel claustrophobic. He was becoming panicky. Could he slip past the two men and out the door? His breathing became faster and deeper. The store manager looked down at him, held out a Milky Way candy bar and said, "I found this on the floor between the racks, just like you told Officer Hancock. I apologize for thinking you stole it. I'd be pleased if you would accept it as my apology." Now confused, Rosey looked at the officer, who nodded his head and smiled for sure this time. Rosey never forgot the incident.

Fifteen years later, when Officer Hancock died, a lonely old man who lived on social security and a small retirement check and had no living relatives, only the funeral director knew it was NFL linebacker Roosevelt Adams who paid for the best casket, a prominent headstone and a grave space in the Odd Fellows cemetery.

Another thing many people do not know is that a Union Medal of Honor winner is also buried in Odd Fellows Cemetery. His name is James Snedden and he was born in 1843 and died in 1919. Snedden was awarded the Congressional Medal of Honor on September 11, 1897, more than thirty-three years after his heroic act. He was a musician in Company E, fifty-fourth Pennsylvania Regiment of the Union forces during the War Between the States. Snedden's citation read, "Left his place in the rear, took the rifle of a disabled soldier, and fought through the remainder of the action." Snedden was mustered out at Harrisburg, Pennsylvania, July 15, 1865, moved to Wyandotte, Kansas, in 1867. He moved to Galena, Kansas, in 1870, where he met and married Mary C. Speck, and in 1875, their only child, Irene M. Snedden, was born. In 1899, Irene Snedden, married Joseph Sessions Eggleston of Holmes County, Mississippi. James and Mary Snedden followed their daughter and her husband back to Holmes County and settled in Lexington. James Snedden passed away on June 18, 1919 at the age of seventy-five and was interred in Odd Fellows Cemetery.

The day after Adams was hired, someone who was a relative newcomer to town and did not know Lexington's history and its people asked the sheriff why he had employed a deputy with no law enforcement experience. The chief just laughed and said to wait until Rosey came back from the state law enforcement training academy. Sure enough, Rosey graduated first in his class. Every once in awhile someone would wonder aloud why Rosey would want to be a law enforcement officer in Holmes County when he probably had millions invested in who knows what all kinds of things, but that subject never got past the wondering stage. Everybody was just glad to have Rosey in town.

Jack Boulder entered the front door of the Holmes County Sheriff's Department and asked to see Chief Deputy Adams. "Go ahead and have a seat in the conference room," the receptionist said. "He will be right with you." Boulder walked around the desk and across the hall to a small conference room. On one wall was a poster-sized frame displaying shoulder patches from police departments around the country. Boulder studied for a moment in search of a patch from St. Louis.

"Mr. Boulder," came a voice behind him. Boulder turned around to see a six-foot seven-inch giant wearing a white police uniform shirt and black pants. The figure filled the doorway.

"You must be Chief Adams?"

"Have a seat, and tell me how I can help you," the Chief Deputy said, motioning toward a chair at the table. The voice was more like a school-teacher instead of James Earl Jones. As they sat down, Boulder noticed how comfortable he felt with this man. When seeing him for the first time, it would be easy to be intimidated, but there was a calming effect in his voice. Boulder imagined how it must be when a driver passing through Lexington was stopped by the police and looked in the rear view mirror to see this colossus getting out of a patrol car.

"I'm trying to learn more about Mildred Monroe, the woman who was killed on Halloween night," Boulder said.

"A most unique woman," Adams said. "Everybody knew her and loved her."

"Was she one of your teachers?"

"No. I didn't go to Saints Academy. I went to public school. But she was well-known. She was sort of ahead of her time."

"In what way?" Boulder asked.

"She always wore pants, even back in the days when women were not supposed to wear pants. I don't think I've ever seen her wear a dress. And she had short hair. She never married as far as I know. Some of the other women talked about her because of that, but everybody liked her. And she always drove a sporty car. She would get a new one about every two years."

"Speaking of her car, I understand it was being carjacked when she was killed?"

"That's right. She was shot in the chest. Apparently, she resisted. The carjacker took her Mustang and led us on a nice little chase. He crashed out on Highway Seventeen just north of the interstate—right in front of the Little Red Schoolhouse.

The shooter is a seventeen-year-old male. He is being charged as an adult. He's been charged with capital murder and carjacking. We have a couple of witnesses who saw him at the scene, and we have Ms. Monroe's blood on one of his shoes."

"Witnesses to the shooting?" Boulder asked.

"Unfortunately, no. A couple of teenagers who heard a shot went to see what was happening and saw two cars leave the St. Paul's church parking lot. They found Ms. Monroe's body beside the parking lot."

"Two cars?"

"Yeah. The other was a black Magnum."

"Do you have many carjackings in Lexington?"

"This is the first one this year."

"Murders?"

"Also the first one this year," Adams said. "Not much in the way of crime here."

"Any ideas on motive?"

"The kid is not talking. My guess is it is probably related to drugs or a gang initiation. Take away drugs and gangs, and we probably would have no need for half the police officers in this country."

"You're probably right," Boulder said. "By the way, there is a possibility that there is more to this. It could be related to another case and just coincidence, but I was followed on the way up here. Here's the tag number. This tag was on the red Mercury that was following me. Can you run a twenty-eight on it?"

"Sure, I'll be right back," Adams said, leaving to inquire about the vehicle registration. He returned shortly. "Man, you know how to get the attention of the big boys."

"Oh really," Boulder said.

"This tag number is registered to a red Mercury owned by Richard Perry, the closest thing around here to an organized crime boss. He owns over a thousand acres in Holmes and

Attala counties and is involved in more shady deals than you could count. Bribery and extortion are his favorite pastimes. He's been arrested twice for extortion, but released after the witnesses disappeared. He's dirty as they come. He's also been suspected of arranging a hit on a former employee who turned on him. One district attorney candidate in the last election ran a campaign on the silent promise he would do something about Richard Perry."

"I take it he didn't win."

"He lost in a close race where several ballot boxes were extremely suspicious." There was a pause while Boulder considered this information. Then Adams asked, "Do you have any reason to believe the carjacking was not a random act?"

"I'm not sure. Conventional wisdom would say someone contacted a gang and ordered a new Mustang or its parts. They find one, steal it and sell it either to the customer or to a chop shop. The really far-fetched idea would be that Mildred Monroe was intentionally murdered, and it was made to look like a carjacking."

"With all due respect, Mr. Boulder, why don't we start over and you tell me why you're really interested in this case."

"Fair enough," Boulder said. "Several people received a letter informing them Mildred Monroe's death was not what it appeared to be. One of them hired me to find out who sent the letter."

"Do you have the letter with you?"

"Sorry, I left it back in Jackson."

"Do you remember who received the letters?"

Boulder consulted his notebook and flipped over the first page, which he always left blank. "They were addressed to Barbara Calhoun, Gregory Greene, Gwendolyn Warren, Reverend Robert Lauderdale and Gus Rankin."

Adams held up a giant hand and extended his fingers. As he called off each name, he used his other hand to lower each finger toward him. "Don't know the first name. Greene went to Saints Academy and now lives in Chicago. Gwen Warren is a social worker in town. Reverend Lauderdale is pastor of Amazing Grace Church. Gus Rankin is a lawyer here in Lexington, and I assume is the one who hired you?"

Boulder let the question about who hired him slide and then said, "I'll make a copy of the letter for you when I get back to Jackson."

"Let me see your notebook," he said reaching his hand across the table. Reluctantly, Boulder handed it to him. Adams retrieved a gold-plated pen from his shirt pocket and wrote on the blank page. "That's my fax number, my office number and my cell phone number. Call me first, and I'll go stand by the fax machine. You can then fax the letter to me."

"Sounds good," Boulder said.

A knock on the door interrupted them. A woman leaned in and said, "Excuse me, Chief. Sounds like a bad accident out on Highway Twelve just inside the city limits." Adams nodded his acknowledgment and stood.

"Duty calls," he said. "Anything else?"

"Two things. One, what age person is this Richard Perry? Two, how do I get to Amazing Grace Church?" Boulder asked.

"Perry is in his mid-sixties," Rosey said. "To get to the church, go back out Highway Seventeen like you're going to Jackson. It's on the right, about three miles from town." As they walked out of the room, Adams added, "And tell the Reverend Lauderdale I want a good prayer Saturday night at the sports banquet."

CHAPTER 10

Reverend Robert Lauderdale paused about halfway between the small, white-frame church and the propane tank in the side yard. He thought he felt dizzy, or maybe he was hot, or cold, or just different than normal. He looked down at his wristwatch and saw that it was 11:30 a.m. Perhaps he just needed to get some food in his stomach. There was a good reason for him to be concerned about his physical condition. His body mass index, or BMI, the measure of body fat based on height and weight, was 38.5. Reverend Lauderdale carried 276 pounds on a frame that stood five feet eleven inches.

He learned of his so-called BMI only two weeks ago when he had visited the health clinic at the University Medical Center in Jackson. The visit was occasioned by his watching television one night and seeing the medical center was offering free health screenings. To him, such an announcement served two purposes. First, he could get a free screening and perhaps even stumble into some research program paying people to be guinea pigs for medical research. Secondly, he would not be seen in the local health clinic by members of his congregation. He had a way of sniffing out good deals and things he could get for free. Finding bargains was an occupational necessity for a pastor in rural Mississippi with a church of only 126 members. His flock did not have enough money to pay him to lead what one would call a comfortable life.

One thing contributing to his BMI was that the reverend seldom paid for food. At least twice during the week and always for Sunday lunch, one church member or another invited him to come to their home for a meal. In this part of the world, it is almost a sin not to invite the pastor to lunch. Actually, in this part of the world—that is to say The South—lunch is referred to as dinner, and dinner is referred to as supper. So a Sunday dinner was almost always guaranteed. And it was also almost always certain he would dine on fried chicken or fried catfish, what with those two items being big crops in Mississippi these days. When he was a young boy, the catfish he ate on were "mudcats," which were bottom feeders caught out of small farm ponds where cattle waded cool off. Nowadays the catfish he dined on were called blue channel catfish and were grown in large, clean ponds in the Mississippi Delta only a few miles to the west.

Reverend Lauderdale's visit to the medical center had not been a success. Indeed, it was a disaster. Just as he walked in the lobby, three women members of his congregation, who were at the medical center visiting a cousin, spotted him in the lobby. They ran up to him and hugged him and thanked him for visiting the sick folks from Lexington who were in the hospital in Jackson. He thanked them and blessed them, and they blissfully strode away. A half hour later they spotted him again, only this time he was in the clinic waiting area holding a number, and they wanted to know why he was there. They were genuinely concerned about his health; he was genuinely concerned about the misrepresentation he had made to them. He realized once again every man was a sinner every day. This took him into such deep thought, he did not hear his number being called until the third loud cry from the receptionist. Once inside an examination room, he was asked a lot of health-related questions, had his blood pressure taken, was stuck in the finger with a needle, and then was generally prodded and poked. When the examination process was complete, the young technician told him he could put his shirt and coat back on and a nurse would be with him momentarily. A few minutes later a middle-aged, stern-looking nurse arrived with clipboard in hand. She studied the clipboard and then sized him up. He was, as always, wearing a black suit, a black shirt and a big, gold cross hanging on a big, gold chain around his big neck. She told him his blood pressure was 150/95 and his sugar level was high enough to classify him a Type II diabetic. Under further questioning, he confessed to her that he had never had a physical examination in his life, which was a lie. When he was admitted to the Mississippi State Penitentiary at Parchman twelve years ago he had a similar examination. She admonished him to see a doctor and gave him a packet of information about the services available to him along with some guides to healthy eating and exercise. He left intent on doing something about his health, but he had yet to do so.

After his "little spell," as his mother would have called it, passed, he walked on toward the propane tank some fifty feet away. He checked the gauge on the tank, looked up at a low, gray, threatening sky and calculated there would be just enough fuel for this coming Sunday's service, but that would be about all. The little building was terribly energy inefficient and sucked the gas like there was no tomorrow. He hoped the credit of the church was still good with the propane service company because there was only $182 left in the church bank account. It costs twice that to fill the tank. As he leaned down and sniffed around the gas lines to make certain there was not a leak, he heard the sound of a vehicle on the gravel parking lot. He looked up and saw a car driving up the front of the church. A man got out of the car and walked toward him.

"Hello, I'm looking for Reverend Lauderdale."

"You found him." They stood six feet apart, sizing each other up.

"I'm Jack Boulder from Jackson. I'm a private investigator." Boulder stuck out his right hand. The reverend accepted it tentatively.

"What can I do for you?"

"I'm here about Mildred Monroe," Boulder said.

"She was a member of my congregation," the reverend said nodding his head affirmatively.

A soft, cold rain began falling, turning Boulder's jacket a darker hue on the shoulders. Reverend Lauderdale stood in place as if he did not notice.

"My client received a letter from someone claiming to be Mildred Monroe. There were four other people listed as recipients. You were one of them.

"Let's go inside. It's starting to rain out here." Boulder followed the pastor as he ambled to the front of the building and then inside, both men now in a stage between damp and wet. The church seated a hundred worshipers in a stark sanctuary on hard, wooden pews donated from another church in town that had replaced them with a cushioned, more contoured variety. A pulpit and two large chairs stood at attention at the front of the worship space. The only other rooms were a unisex restroom and a storage closet. There were no stained glass windows, no baptistery and no altar. The setting was purely functional for listening to a sermon. They walked down the center aisle to the first row, where the pastor motioned for Boulder to have a seat. Boulder noticed it was colder inside the church than it was outside. They sat on the front row facing each other, each draping an arm over the back of the pew. Boulder spoke first.

"These letters were supposedly mailed to the members of the Fifty-K Club." Boulder paused and let the sentence rest in the space between them. Silence and a waiting stare were sometimes the best questions. The other man moved his hand from the back of the pew to his chin and rubbed it as if he were checking to see if he needed to shave. His eyes moved away from Boulder and gazed up toward the pulpit. He took a slightly wheezy deep breath and spoke.

"I'm not a member of the Fifty-K Club," he said defensively.

"Why do you think your name is on the list?"

"Because I'm the pastor of the church," he replied, his voice rising.

"So the church is a member of the Fifty-K Club?"

Reverend Lauderdale reacted instantly. "Who did you say was your client?"

"I didn't," Boulder said. The sound of rain hitting the roof could now be heard overhead.

"May I see your identification?"

Boulder reached in his pocket and handed the other man one of his business cards. It contained only Boulder's name and telephone number.

"As I said earlier, I am a private investigator."

"I guess your client is one of the people on the list like me."

"That would be a logical deduction," Boulder said, raising his head and scanning the room. "Tell me about your church."

"What?" Reverend Lauderdale said. "Oh, my church. About a hundred and twenty-five souls who love the Lord and are saved by the grace of Jesus Christ."

"How long have you been their pastor?"

"Going on three years now," the reverend replied.

Boulder did some mental math and figured there was no way a small rural church in Mississippi could compensate a full-time pastor, pay the utility bills and be a member of the Fifty-K Club. "Is this your only job?" Boulder asked.

"Yes," the reverend replied. His answer was not the whole truth; it was not completely an untruth either. What Reverend Robert Lauderdale did not reveal was that he made more money on the side singing the *Star Spangled Banner* at public events than he did preaching at this little church. His singing ability had been discovered five years ago by the governor during a visit to Parchman. Lauderdale's gift of song was well-known in the penitentiary, so the warden had him open a luncheon for the governor with a gospel hymn. The governor eventually had him sing at his second inauguration. Robert Lauderdale looked and sang like Barry White. He was heavy, had long hair and possessed a deep and seductive voice. He also had a look in his eye that said he knew things others did not. He was so good at the statewide televised swearing-in ceremony, large business associations and corporations subsequently paid him between $200 and $400 to open their meetings. He always sang either the *Star Spangled Banner* or his stirring version of the *Lord's Prayer*. The payments were always made in cash or a check payable to him personally. No one in his church knew he did these activities on the side.

"It's none of my business, but how do you do it?" Boulder asked. "There must be a rich church member somewhere in there that does more than merely tithe his fair share."

"No sir," the pastor said. "Out that opaque window there is a little single-wide mobile home and a fifteen-year-old Buick. They are all I need for what I do, which is to minister to the folks who come to this church. I get by with the help of the Lord." He paused, pulled out a handkerchief and coughed twice into it. "You believe in God, don't you..." he looked down at the business card in his hand ... "Mr. Jack Boulder?"

"No offense, Reverend Lauderdale, but I like to keep my religious beliefs to myself."

"So you don't believe in God?"

"I did not say that."

"So you do believe in God?"

"I didn't say that either," Boulder said.

The pastor gave up the line of inquiry into his visitor's faith. At least for the moment. "Now what do you want to know?"

"Let's begin with Mildred Monroe."

"Bless her heart and soul," he replied. "She was a rock and a strong believer, she was. I wish more people had her faith."

"How long had she been a member of your church?"

"She was one of the originals. I guess the church had been open for about a month when she came in. She just walked in one Sunday morning and sat down on the second row over there. She made quite a fuss with some of the women because Mildred Monroe wore pants and she did not wear a hat."

"Why is that important?" Boulder asked.

"Most women in this church believe when you come to church you are presenting yourself before the Lord, and you should look your best. A lot of these women were taught that a woman should have her head covered when she comes into church. It's in Paul's first letter to the Corinthians, in chapter five if you want to look it up. Anyway, because Miss Mildred did not wear a hat, she was immediately looked down upon. But I think that was just what she wanted. She was always challenging people, challenging them to do better, to be better than they were. I think not wearing a hat and wearing pants was her way of making people think about why they do the things they do."

"I understand," Boulder said with a nod. "Just one more question."

"And that would be?"

"Did you get a letter?"

"I believe I did," Reverend Lauderdale said.

"Do you still have it?"

"No sir. Threw it away."

"Did you tell anybody about it?" Boulder asked.

"Can't say as I did."

"With all due respect, Reverend. I'm trying hard to understand why you would throw away a letter supposedly from a member of your congregation who was deceased."

"Because it was a prank," Reverend Lauderdale replied. "A sick joke. I prayed for the person who wrote it." There was an uncomfortable pause between the two men. Finally, Reverend Lauderdale said, "Any more questions?"

"That's all," Boulder said. "Thank you for your time. You've been very helpful." Boulder started to stand up, but realized in the middle of his arising that the pastor remained seated. He awkwardly sat back down.

"Do you mind if I ask YOU a few questions?" the pastor asked.

"Of course not," Boulder said, remembering a good interviewer always concludes an interview by asking, "Is there anything else you want to tell me?"

"Are you a religious man, Mr. Boulder?"

"What do you mean?"

"Do you believe in God?" the elder asked softly. "Do you go to church? Do you pray?"

Boulder turned slightly in his chair and said, "Yes, I believe in God." He paused and stared at the elder's bookcase. "I do not go to church as much as I should." Another pause, this time Boulder's eyes slipped a glance at the ceiling. "And I pray from time to time."

"Are you saved?"

"I beg your pardon?"

"Have you accepted Jesus Christ as your personal Savior?"

"Well, with all due respect, I think that's sort of a personal question," Boulder said.

"Oh my God, Man! You haven't accepted Jesus Christ as your personal Savior, have you?" It was as if he had discovered Jack Boulder was someone else in disguise. He moved as if he was about to stand up.

"Now Reverend Lauderdale..."

"No. Wait," he said, holding his hands up, palms extended toward Boulder. The reverend took a deep breath, calmed himself and spoke deliberately. "If you walked out that door back there and saw a little child, a little baby child, sitting right in the middle of the highway, and a big eighteen wheeler was coming down the road, what would you do?

"Grab the child and get it out of the road, I suppose."

"Suppose nothing," the pastor said, becoming animated and using his hands. "You would risk your life to pick up that child and save it from certain death."

"I wouldn't disagree with that," Boulder replied.

"Just like that little child you would save, I would not let you go to hell if I could save you." Reverend Lauderdale stood up and moved to one of the chairs behind the pulpit. He kneeled in front of the chair, placed his elbows on the seat and clasped his hands. He lowered his head and closed his eyes. Boulder watched as this big hunk of a preacher presumably prayed. There was a sniffle. Was the preacher catching a cold from being out in the rain? Three minutes later—it seemed like ten to Boulder—the pastor stood up, wiped his cheeks with his handkerchief and then sat back down on the front row. "Mr. Boulder, I believe if a person has not accepted Jesus Christ as his personal Savior, he will spend eternity in hell. Because I believe that way, it is important for me to know whether every person I meet is saved or not. That is why I have to ask them. If they are not saved I have to do everything in my power to save them."

"What about the Jews, the Muslims, the other religions and the babies who do not know enough to be saved?"

"I'll be honest with you, Mr. Boulder. I really do not know. I wish I could answer that question because it is asked a lot. All I know is what I must do. I could not sleep tonight if I thought I had not tried to save you from eternal damnation."

"I confess that I admire your dedication," Boulder said seriously.

"You've got all the pastors nowadays saying they want to respect everybody's beliefs. You've got pastors who say they do not want to offend anybody because of what they believe.

Well I say if you believe in the Bible, you will offend some people some of the time. The Bible is clear on one point. There is only one way to heaven and that is through Jesus Christ. People around here say I am a little crazy for believing what I believe, but if you look at what is said in the pulpits all across America, you will find preachers are saying they believe the same thing. It is obvious they do not believe it because they are not doing it."

"I understand your point," Boulder said.

The pastor sat back down and looked at Boulder as a psychiatrist would look at a patient. He had done this before. He had an uncanny ability to know when people wanted to keep talking. Most people are reluctant to tell a pastor what they really feel; they want to tell the pastor what they think the pastor wants to hear. Then there will come a point in the conversation where the need to reveal overrides the need to please. The reverend felt Boulder was almost at that point.

"It's just that I sort of get uncomfortable talking about religion, if you know what I mean."

"And I understand your point," Reverend Lauderdale said. He closed his eyes. That funny feeling was coming over him again. A strange dizziness. Silently, he asked for strength.

"Are you all right?"

Lauderdale opened his eyes and nodded. He took a deep breath. "Who's the next person on your list?"

"Gwendolyn Warren."

"She can tell you a lot about Mildred Monroe."

"Thank you, sir," Boulder said, and stood.

Reverend Lauderdale remained seated and waved him away. Was his left arm becoming numb?

CHAPTER 11

Boulder ran through the rain across crunchy gravel and plopped into the rental car. He pulled out his notebook and looked at the list of names. Chief Deputy Adams said he did not know Barbara Calhoun, but the other female on the list, Gwendolyn Warren, was a social worker in town. Boulder decided that because he was already in the area, he might as well attempt to make contact with her. Gregory Greene had said she was some kind of doctor. Boulder decided the best place to find somebody without eliciting a lot of questions was the local library. There he could use the Internet and a local telephone book. He started the car, turned on the windshield wipers and headlights and drove back to Lexington.

In a few moments, Boulder arrived at the town square. Like many town squares in Mississippi, there was a courthouse in the middle of the square. Lexington's Courthouse was built around 1894 and was designed by architect W. Chamberlin & Co. It is a Mississippi Landmark building. The structure combines elements of both the Romanesque and the Queen Anne styles. A rectangular, two-story, red-brick structure with tan brick and stone trim, it is bilaterally symmetrical. It was designed with entrances on all four sides, each side facing on the four points of the compass. At each corner is a square, pyramidal roof tower projecting slightly from each wall plane. A tall, working clock tower dominates the building at the center of the roof atop a polygonal dome capped by a lantern and weathervane. Each facade of the building is centered on a tetra-style portico, the columns of which are cast iron. The building was completely renovated in 2004.

Boulder drove around until he found the library two blocks north of the Square on the corner of Tchula and Pine Streets. He went inside and wandered around a few minutes before settling in to his task. Without ever opening a book, a local library can be a good source for getting the feel and history of a town and its people. Most have historic photographs and articles posted about. Boulder saw a photograph of a woman and an article about her underneath. He began reading. Lexington had a Pulitzer Prize winner?

Hazel Brannon Smith
1914-1994

Journalist Hazel Freeman Brannon Smith, the first woman to receive the Pulitzer Prize for editorial writing, was born in 1914 in Gadsden, Alabama, where she graduated from high school in 1930 at the age of sixteen. She graduated from the University of Alabama in 1935 with a B.A. in Journalism.

In 1935, she moved to Durant, MS and bought the failing *Durant News*, and in 1943 she purchased the *Lexington Advertiser*, which she edited and published from 1943 to 1983. In 1956, she acquired the *Banner County Outlook* and the *Northside Reporter.*

Smith's editorials and her column ("Through Hazel's Eyes") focused on unpopular causes, political corruption and social injustice in Mississippi.

Her opposition to the white Citizens' Council brought her the Pulitzer Prize for editorial writing in 1964 for her "steadfast adherence to her editorial duty in the face of great pressure and opposition."

She received awards from the National Federation of Press Women (1946, 1955), the Herrick Award for Editorial Writing (1956), the Mississippi Press Association (1957) and the National Federation of Press Women. She was one of the subjects in the documentary film *An Independent Voice* (1973) about small-town newspaper editors, and her life was dramatized in the TV movie *A Passion for Justice: The Hazel Brannon Smith Story* (1994). A biography of Smith was written by John Whalen entitled *Maverick Among the Magnolias*. She died in Cleveland, TN in 1994.

Boulder signed in to use a computer and then settled in for some Internet research. Pulling up a search engine, he typed in the tag number of the car that had been following him. As he suspected, there were no matches found. He knew it would not be long before a tag number could be entered into an Internet search engine and the vehicle owner's information would appear. Already, it was possible to enter a telephone number and get several hits if the number was listed in a telephone book or if the number was posted on some website as contact information. He entered "Gwendolyn Warren" in the space provided on the screen. He hoped for an address and telephone number. When he saw the results of his search on the screen, he almost fell back in his chair. He took a deep breath, exhaled slowly and looked around as if making sure no one had seen him make his surprising discovery. There were pages and pages of information about Dr. Gwendolyn Warren, "someone who gave up a promising career to return to her hometown and serve others." He discovered personal interviews, magazine websites, news articles about awards she had received and several stories about inspiring speeches she had delivered at various schools. Boulder's eyes widened as he read page after page. After thirty-five minutes of reading, he leaned back and digested all the pieces of information in front of him about the woman's life story.

Gwendolyn Warren grew up in Lexington, the daughter of a mother who worked as a waitress at a truck stop on the interstate and a father who could not keep a job because of alcoholism. She attended Saints Academy in Lexington and then earned a college degree at Millsaps College, where she was elected class president her senior year. She followed up with a masters and then Ph.D. in Behavioral Sciences at Emory University in Atlanta, Georgia. Several articles depicted her volunteer work in Atlanta in community mental health and youth projects. Following graduation she was employed by a large, private, mental-health facility in suburban Atlanta. After several years she decided to return to Mississippi and work in her hometown of Lexington.

Boulder studied a photograph of her and guessed she was at least five-feet nine-inches tall. She looked like a model for a beauty product. Indeed, she was strikingly beautiful, almost glamorous. Boulder found no evidence she had ever been married. According to a local newspaper article, she was in private practice in an office on Depot Street and had consulting relationships with several hospitals and the State Department of Corrections. He wrote down the address in his notebook, found the location on an Internet mapping site, and headed back out into the rain. It was 1:20 p.m. when he pulled up in front of her office.

CHAPTER 12

The receptionist sitting at a small desk in a small and modestly furnished room greeted him. Behind her was a framed copy of Gwendolyn Warren's Doctorate of Philosophy. Otherwise, the walls held only framed prints that looked like they had been purchased at a furniture store. Boulder introduced himself and asked to speak to Dr. Warren.

"Do you have an appointment?" the receptionist asked as she consulted a large calendar laying flat on her desk.

"No. I was hoping to catch her between appointments."

"Just one moment," the receptionist said. "May I ask what it is in reference to?"

"It's about Mildred Monroe."

The receptionist gave him a curious look, as if trying to decide if he was a salesman, and then excused herself. Momentarily, she returned and said, "Dr. Warren will see you now." She motioned him back into a short hallway with a low ceiling. Boulder noticed a conference room on his right. There were about ten chairs in a circle in the middle of the room. This was definitely Class B, functional office space. Dr. Gwendolyn Warren, looking professional in a dark skirt and a light blue blouse, appeared in a doorway to his left. She was as beautiful in person as she was in the photos he had seen on the Internet, even though she wore little, if any, makeup.

"I understand you are here to see me about Mildred Monroe?"

"Yes," Boulder replied. "Do you have a few minutes?"

She looked down at her wristwatch, and said, "Looks like my one o'clock has decided not to get out in the rain." She opened her door and motioned him to a chair sitting in front of a large desk. Her office was as basic as the rest of the place. There was one window looking out onto the parking lot. She sat down in another chair beside him. Boulder was not accustomed to people he interviewed sitting beside him. In such situations most would go behind the desk so as to put as much of a barrier as possible between them. She seemed comfortable, he thought. Then again, she should. She was a psychologist, or social worker, or something along those lines. She crossed her legs and pushed her skirt toward her knees. Boulder tried to avoid looking down. He introduced himself by name and handed her a business card. She did not react.

"I assume you are familiar with the Fifty-K Club," Boulder said.

"Oh yes. Miss Monroe pushed hard to get that started."

"Who else was in the club?"

"I don't know all of the members," she said. "It was a small group. Less than ten people, I think. What's this about?"

"Do you know Gregory Greene?"

"Of course I do. We were in the same class at Saints."

"And was he a member of the Fifty-K Club?"

"Yes."

"Did you receive a letter from Miss Monroe around Thanksgiving about the Fifty-K Club?"

"Yes, I did. It was a thank you letter."

"Did it seem strange to you to receive a letter from someone who had died a month earlier?"

"I must admit is was an odd feeling when I opened it, but I just assumed someone had mailed it for her. She was very organized. It would not have surprised me to learn she had written it in September and laid it on her desk to be mailed come Thanksgiving. She would do that sometimes. She would address and seal Christmas cards all year, stack them on her desk and then mail them out in December. You know I don't remember if I even read the entire letter. When I saw it was a thank you letter, I put it down. I'm not trying to avoid the question, I just really don't remember."

"Do you still have the letter?"

"I'm sure I've thrown it away by now."

"Was there anything unusual about the letter?"

"Not that I recall," she said. "It was just a nice thank you letter."

"When did you last see her?"

"I guess it would have been the day before she was killed. I saw her coming out of BankPlus on the Square. She waved and got into that red Mustang of hers." Dr. Warren moved her hands into a steeple position. "What is your interest in Miss Monroe? Are you with her insurance company?"

"No. I was hired to find out who sent the letters from Lexington to Gregory Greene, Gus Rankin, Reverend Lauderdale, Barbara Calhoun and you."

"Would you care to tell me who hired you?" she asked.

"I'm afraid I need to keep my client's name confidential."

"It was either Gregory or Ms. Calhoun, wasn't it?

"Like I said..."

"Don't worry," she said. "You don't have to answer. It's so obvious anyway."

"How do you figure that?"

"Process of elimination. Reverend Lauderdale would not have enough money to hire a private investigator. Gus Rankin lives in Lexington and has his own resources to discover something like that. I did not hire you. Gregory and Ms. Calhoun live out of town and have enough money to hire anybody to do anything."

"Tell me about Ms. Calhoun," Boulder said.

"She's a widow who lives in Jackson. Her husband, Clarence Calhoun, had been making an annual contribution to Saints College for years. The school recruited his money and support years ago. When Saints closed a couple of years ago, Miss Monroe called on him to contribute to the Save Our Saints Foundation. He died recently, so who knows if Ms. Calhoun will keep making the contribution."

"And Gregory Greene?"

"Grey, as he now likes to be called, lives in Chicago. He's a television personality and a wealthy businessman. The television personality part did not surprise any of us. He was always outgoing, in school plays, that sort of thing. Most of us in his class were surprised to see he even graduated at all. The director wanted to suspend him from school, but Miss Monroe convinced her to let him stay."

"What happened?"

"He went home with one of his buddies in north Mississippi one weekend. Nine months later, a girl and her aunt showed up at school and claimed Gregory was the father of her new child. Rumor had it that Gregory's father paid off the family."

"Was Saints a boarding school?"

"Oh, yes. Even those of us who were from Lexington lived on campus. But there were students and teachers from all over the world."

"Where was Gregory Greene from?"

"He was from Chicago. Another rumor was that he had a choice of being sent to reform school or coming to Saints. Anyway, we thought he might wind up on television in Jackson, not in a big city like Chicago. But it did not surprise Miss Monroe at all. She always told us we could be even bigger than our dreams."

"Was that true in your case?"

She turned her head, but her eyes stayed on her visitor. "And what does that mean?"

"Nothing sinister intended," Boulder said. "I looked on the Internet for your address and stumbled onto a lot of information about Doctor Gwendolyn Warren. I admire your dedication to your hometown. What made you come back?"

She stood and walked over to the window, turning her back on him. He heard a sniffle. A moment passed. She turned and pulled a tissue out of a box on her desk. She sat back down and wiped away soft tears. "It's usually my clients who need the tissues, I'm afraid." Boulder said nothing. "I came back because Miss Monroe came to Atlanta and told me I was needed in Lexington. She talked about how kids were losing their way nowadays and how adults needed someone to talk to. You know, in Atlanta I felt needed and I knew I was needed, but no one there ever TOLD me they needed me. Miss Monroe invoked the life of Dr. Mallory. After that, I could not say no."

"Dr. Mallory?" Boulder asked.

"You have never heard of Dr. Mallory?"

"Sorry, but I haven't," he said. "Please educate me." She then told him the story of Dr. Arenia Mallory, founder and leader of Saints Industrial and Literacy School, later known as Saints Junior College and Saints Academy.

Dr. Arenia Mallory was born in Jacksonville, Illinois in 1905. In 1927, she earned a bachelor's degree from Simmons College of Kentucky; later, a master's degree from Jackson State University; in 1950, a master's degree from the University of Illinois; and in 1951, a doctorate of law from Bethune-Cookman College. Mallory founded Saints Industrial and Literary School in Lexington, Mississippi. The historically black school was renamed to Saints Academy. She served as president of the school from 1926 until her death in 1983. It was operated under auspices of the Church of God in Christ. Mallory was an active member of the Church of God in Christ, becoming leader of the Women's Department in the national church. She served as the Vice President of the National Council of Negro Women from 1953-1957, was a member of the Regional Council of Negro Leadership, a consultant for the United States Department of Labor in 1963, and the first woman and first African-American elected to the Holmes County Board of Education. Mallory also has two facilities named after her—the Dr. Arenia C. Mallory Community Health Center in Lexington, Mississippi, and the Arenia Mallory-Albany School of Religion located in Miami, Florida. Dr. Arenia C. Mallory Community Health Center (MCHC) is named to honor her memory as a well known educator and champion of human causes. She inspired young minds regardless of their race, economic or social status to "Walk in Dignity, Talk in Dignity, and Live in Dignity." She is remembered by her former students as a woman of high integrity, establishing loving but strong discipline, and a teacher of the highest caliber.

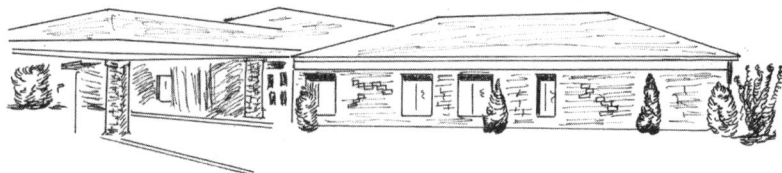

CHAPTER 13

Boulder drove back to the Square, this time coming in on Depot Street, where the last quarter mile before the center of town was a curvy, hilly road lined with colorful banners on telephone poles extolling the city. The streets were still wet, but the rain had let up. He negotiated the drive around the Courthouse to the south side of the Square where Attorney Gus Rankin's office was located a few doors down from the Justice Court office. He pulled in a space in front of Holmes County Bank and Trust and walked back to Rankin's office, having more questions in mind for the attorney than any other of the persons he had interviewed so far or planned to interview. His mission was foiled, however, when Rankin's assistant told him the attorney was in court in another county and would not be back until Thursday. Boulder managed a frustrated smile and left word for Rankin to call him on his cell phone when he returned.

Boulder walked outside and felt a large raindrop hit the top of his head. The sky to the west was looking darker. He decided it might to be a good idea to invest in an umbrella. Across the way, he saw a sign on a corner building reading "Peoples Drug Store." He made his way to the establishment just before the rain came down. Inside, he was greeted by a smiling, middle-aged woman who said, "Hello. Can I help you?"

The interior of the store was not what he expected. In the larger cities where he's lived, there were mostly chain drug stores with bright, fluorescent lights and employees who seldom, if ever, ask customers what they need. It had occurred to him recently that the three large chain stores in Jackson all carry the same items, which are stacked on high shelves defining narrow aisles. Peoples Drug Store exhibits no such characteristics. The ceiling, covered with original pressed tin tiles, must be fifteen feet high. The only semblance of gridded aisles is in back of the store where the health and beauty items are found. In the far back of the store, the pharmacy is raised a foot above floor level of the rest of the store. The front two-thirds of the establishment resembles an upscale department emporium, which should not be surprising in view of the fact that there are items ranging from decorative candles to jewelry to clothing to gifts. There is even a section dedicated to Ole Miss and Mississippi State paraphernalia. The retail lines include Vera Bradley Handbags and Luggage, Gail Pittman Pottery, Southern Belle T-shirts, and a host of baby and children gifts available for gift-wrapping or monogramming at the store.

"I'm in the market for an umbrella," Boulder said.

"Follow me," the clerk replied, and led him to an area with various styles and types of umbrellas. He picked the cheapest, black one he could find. She checked him out at the cash register and bid him Godspeed. Boulder walked back out on the sidewalk, pausing under the store's canopy as the rain pelted the covering overhead. He looked across the street to the Courthouse, and saw a young man running through the rain to a row of parked cars. He thought the man should not be running so fast, lest he slip and fall on the wet pavement. The man partially disappeared into a row of cars, only his shoulder and head visible. He got into a vehicle. Seconds later, a small blue car backed out into the interior lane of the Square. Boulder froze, his umbrella halfway unfolded. The car was his 1968 Chevy Camaro.

CHAPTER 14

Boulder threw the umbrella to the ground, dashed across the street and stood squarely in the path of the car. He held his hand up, military-police-style. The Camaro stopped less than a foot in front of him. Boulder walked around to the driver's side window, rain now coming down harder. The driver rolled the window down two inches.

"Whose car is this?" Boulder demanded.

"What's it to you?" came the reply.

"Get out of the car," Boulder said, reaching down and pulling open the driver's door.

The driver immediately accelerated, causing the door to slam shut and the back end of the car to slide sideways. The Camaro started speeding away, its rear tires spinning. Boulder looked around for any assistance he could find. He saw it coming straight at him from the north. The sheriff's department patrol car was within fifty feet when he started waving his arms back and forth, looking like some crazy athlete doing jumping jacks in the rain. As the car pulled up beside him, Boulder ran for the passenger side door and jumped in. Chief Deputy Rosey Adams looked at him with wide eyes. Boulder was soaked.

"That's my car," Boulder said, pointing at the Camaro, which was now on the opposite side of the Square and making a turn to the north.

"Buckle up," Adams instructed.

Adams pressed on the accelerator hard, but not hard enough to make the car spin sideways on the wet street. He flipped the switch to turn on the blue lights and the siren. The Ford Crown Victoria Police Interceptor responded accordingly. Everyone around the Square looked in the direction of the siren, watching as Adams negotiated the lanes between parked cars on both sides and then disappeared north on Highway 12 from the Square. The Camaro was already almost a quarter mile ahead. The Camaro approached the intersection of Highways 12 and 17, an unusual intersection in that a vehicle approaching from the south that kept going straight would suddenly be on Highway 17 North while the main road curved toward the west. The other problem for the Camaro was that the maximum speed one could negotiate the curve was severely reduced when the road was wet. Consequently, the Camaro slid sideways through the intersection onto Highway 17 North. It then spun completely around and stopped. The driver recovered, started the car, and headed north once again as the patrol car closed in. The rear end of the Camaro slid from side to side on the wet road as the driver fought to keep from losing control. The car turned right on Bryan Street, the sheriff's department's car now hugging its rear bumper, and then right again on North Street. The wet street and the pursuing patrol car were too much for the driver. He overcorrected and ran into the ditch in front of the Noel House, the historic mansion named for a former Mississippi governor from Lexington.

Now immobile in the ditch, the driver abandoned the car and fled on foot onto the grounds of the stately mansion. Adams was on his radio informing the dispatcher the subject vehicle had crashed and he was now in pursuit on foot. Even though Adams was a former NFL player and Boulder was a middle-aged jogger in good physical shape, they were no match for the now-fleeing driver, a young man who was darting like a rabbit for the cover of the bushes and shrubs adjacent to the main house which sits on a hill over sixty yards from the street. Within minutes, the property was surrounded by Lexington Police and Holmes County law enforcement personnel. Adams used his handheld radio.

"Dispatch," he barked. "Call the residents of the Noel House and tell them to lock the doors and not to open them to anyone not wearing a uniform."

CHAPTER 15

The Noel House, which is located at 315 North Street, is identified as such because it was the home of Edmond F. Noel, the thirty-seventh governor of Mississippi. He was born near Lexington on March 4, 1856. After attending high school in Louisville, Kentucky, he studied law and was admitted to the bar in 1877, when he began his legal career in his hometown of Lexington. Between 1881 and 1903, he held a number of elected positions, including state representative, district attorney and state senator. While a member of the Mississippi State Senate from 1895 to 1903, he authored the Mississippi primary election law, as well as the "Noel" amendment which made all elective offices four-year terms. In 1907, Noel ran for Governor as a democrat and was elected. He was sworn into office on January 21, 1908. During his tenure, a state livestock sanitary board was formed; a child labor law was sanctioned, as well as a pure food law; a teacher's college was planned at Hattiesburg; an agricultural high school system was created; a state charity hospital at Jackson was established; and a statewide prohibition law was authorized. After completing his term, Noel left office on January 16, 1912. He continued to stay politically active, winning reelection to the Mississippi State Senate, a position he held from 1920 until his death. Governor Edmond F. Noel died on July 30, 1927, and was buried in the Odd Fellows Cemetery.

The house was built in 1875 by John Edgar Gwin, a prominent landowner and attorney. Mr. Gwin lived there until his death in 1898. His estate conveyed the house to Mrs. Margaret

Ann Noel, the mother of Edmond Favor Noel. E. F. Noel inherited the house at the death of his mother in 1904. During his ownership, it is said that Governor Noel played host to President Theodore Roosevelt when "Teddy" was in the area for his now legendary bear hunt near Onward, which is located in the Mississippi Delta. When Noel married Alice Tye Neilson of Pickens, Mississippi in 1905, she named the estate "Oak Hill." The house is an outstanding example of the Late-Victorian Queen-Anne style of architecture modified in the early twentieth century into the Neo-Classical style. It faces west from the center of a deep, landscaped yard fronting North Street.

Its hipped and gabled roof is covered by the cementitious slate from its early twentieth century remodeling. Its facade is five bays wide, with a two-story hip-roofed porch on the center and left bays. The porch has massive wooden Ionic columns under an entablature with metopes and dentil molding on a plain frieze with a layered base. The porte cochere and the balcony are supported on smaller reeded, wooden Ionic columns with molded bases. Engaged columns at the porch edges are half-columns. The gabled wing at the right of the facade has tripartite windows at both levels and a fixed, circular light in a surround with a molded top and keystone centered in the gable. The home remained in the Noel/Neilson family until it was sold to an investor and subsequently to Pat Barrett, Jr.

in 1989, who completely renovated it. He and his wife Janice have recently completed additional renovation work and open it occasionally to visiting tour groups.

It took almost an hour, but the car thief was finally discovered shivering under the front porch of the Noel House in an area offering excellent concealment. It had, in fact, been scanned several times. The operation encompassed twenty law enforcement personnel and an equal number of volunteers. The grounds of the Noel Estate looked like an adult version of an Easter egg hunt.

While the others were doing the searching, Jack Boulder took the opportunity to examine his Camaro. The car's front was pointed downward in the ditch like a dog pawing in a hole for a rodent. The back end was partially in the street, one of the rear wheels resting on pavement and the other hovering three inches above the asphalt. There was some body damage to the front end and the front wheel appeared to be bent out of alignment. The interior of the car looked as good as when Boulder last saw it. There was no sign of litter or abuse inside the car. He removed the key from the ignition and opened the trunk, where he had left a Global Positioning System (GPS) tracking system laying in the open. Unbelievably, the device was still there. He had used it several times to track subject vehicles in cases he was investigating. It was especially useful in divorce cases. The system could be wired to the radio under the dash and then tracked using the Internet. The device had cost less than five hundred dollars at an electronics store and had paid for itself many times over. GPS trackers were primarily used by trucking companies so company management could monitor their big rigs. The devices showed speed, direction of travel and could issue alerts if a driver drove out of a certain zone. Parents of teenagers were beginning to discover the devices as well and install them in the family car or the teenager's car. Boulder's next purchase was going to be a new GPS tracking device which did not need to be wired to the vehicle's electrical system. The electronics market was coming out with new tracking and monitoring products just about every day. A private investigator had to watch out, or he could easily overspend on technology.

He reached in to pick up the gadget and saw something dark resting against the back of the rear seat. There, just behind the GPS tracker, was a black semi-automatic pistol.

CHAPTER 16

Boulder looked up toward the Noel House and saw Adams and another officer escorting a handcuffed individual down the winding driveway. The arrestee wore blue jeans, tennis shoes and a hooded jacket. He had black hair and light brown skin. Boulder guessed he was of Latin descent. Adams shoved the prisoner in the back of the other deputy's car and instructed him to take the subject to the sheriff's office. "I'll be there in a minute," Adams told his officer.

The rain had let up again and the clouds were turning lighter. The temperature was dropping as the wind started to pick up. It was now mid-afternoon. Those who had joined in the hunt for a fleeing car thief were beginning to disburse, making their way back to pickups and SUV's parked on either side of North Street, which had effectively become a one-lane road. Some hung around to talk to acquaintances they had not seen in a while and to catch up on local gossip and current events. For many, it had been an hour of excitement in an otherwise calm small town. They would now go home and tell family and friends about their inside knowledge of the chase and capture of a fleeing criminal. Some would embellish their roles in the event, while others would downplay their's.

In a small town like Lexington this was big and exciting news, especially because it started right there on the Square where so many Christmas shoppers, merchants and others had heard the sirens and witnessed the beginning of the chase. That so many had the opportunity to play a part would make the story of the chase even more dramatic. It was vintage human nature. As the bard said, "All the world's a stage, and all the men and women merely players."

Adams walked over to Boulder, studied the Camaro and grinned, "Looks like you got your car back in one piece, more or less."

"I've got something else," Boulder said. "Take a look at this." He leaned inside the trunk and pointed to the gun.

Adams removed his pen from his shirt pocket and stuck it through the trigger guard. He gently slid the pistol up the tilted trunk floor. Keeping the pen through the trigger guard, he picked up the pistol, stepped over to his patrol car and laid the weapon on the hood. He leaned down and inspected it further. He then reached in his holster, pulled out his service pistol and laid it beside the other one. They were virtually identical.

"Glock Seventeen," Adams said. "Now I wonder where this could have come from." Because of its reliability, light weight and magazine capacity, the Glock 17 is one of the top choices in sidearms for law enforcement agencies in the United States. The model 17 is not designated as such because its magazine carries seventeen rounds of ammunition, but is so named because it carries the seventeenth patent obtained by the Gaston Glock Company. Much of the weapon is made of polymer, although the barrel, slide and some internal parts are made of metal. Adams held his portable radio to his mouth and said, "Dispatch, this is S.O. two."

"Go ahead, S.O. two."

"Go to secure channel, please." He reached down and twisted a knob on top of the radio and said, "I've got a Glock Seventeen firearm. Run this serial number and advise if reported stolen." He dictated the serial number slowly. "Also, go ahead and dispatch the nearest available tow truck."

The two men made a closer inspection of the car and found nothing unusual. Adams took down the vehicle identification number. They made small talk as they waited. The tow truck arrived in twelve minutes. Adams and the driver greeted each other. As the operator hooked a chain to the rear axle of the Camaro to pull it out of the ditch, Boulder asked him to be gentle with it. Boulder and Adams went to the sheriff's office.

"I'm going to be busy awhile with our new guest," Adams said. "You want to check back with me in an hour?"

"Sure," Boulder said. "My rental car is parked on the Square. I'll just browse around and do a little Christmas shopping and come back about four."

CHAPTER 17

Boulder walked the short block to the Square and window-shopped along the west side. He heard the noise of a diesel engine and looked ahead to see a tour bus pull alongside the curb on the southwest side of the Square. Out of curiosity, he strolled toward the bus only to see it pull away and depart to the south. Where it had stopped, there was a sign on the building reading, "Lexington Main Street Association." Looking through a large, plate-glass window, he saw a woman setting a clipboard and some papers on a desk. He decided to check it out. As he walked in, a man he hadn't noticed through the window walked toward him. The man paused and turned to the woman and said, "Next time I want to see the boat."

"We will work something out," said the woman

"Hello," she said warmly. "May I help you?"

"I'm from Jackson and have about an hour to kill. Do you have any suggestions?"

"Of course," she laughed. "Spend a lot of money." She reached down and picked up several brochures. "Seriously, here are some brochures about our town. I suggest you just walk around the Square. You'll find some really good stores, and you can't beat Kittrells' on the Square Restaurant if you plan on being here at dinner."

"Was that a tour bus that just left?"

"Yes, that was a senior citizens group from Jackson. One of our Lexingtonians has organized a tour of our historic churches in Lexington. She leads groups who come into town to see them." She handed him a brochure. "We're getting famous for our churches. Take a look."

Jack Boulder looked down at the pamphlet in his hand. It was entitled "Historic Church Tour, Lexington, Mississippi, hosted by the Lexington Main Street Association." Inside he found a listing of churches and brief descriptions of each. He read the pamphlet slowly.

ASIA BAPTIST CHURCH

Asia Baptist Church was organized in 1871 after the merging of two groups of people—Mt. Pleasant which spent many years worshipping "under a brush arbor" and Asia Missionary Baptist Church.

With this great victory won, they realized that in order to move forward and be successful doing God's work, they needed a strong and determined administration.

The pioneer pastor of this great group of worshipers was Rev. R. G. Moody, pastoring from 1871 to 1903. During the pastorate of R. B. Gayden, the first Men & Women's Day Program, Old Folks Day Program, and Youth Day Program were established.

A two-story brick and stone educational building of sixteen rooms was added to the existing church complex and dedicated in 1945 under the leadership of Rev. A. L. Hill.

FIRST BAPTIST CHURCH

On September 1, 1846, the Baptist Church of Lexington was organized with twenty-two members.

Soon after the congregation was organized in 1846, Mr. Otha Beall donated the lot upon which the church now stands. Immediately, a small frame building was erected which served the church until 1890, when the current sanctuary was constructed. The 1890 building had a balcony and four Sunday School rooms; when the building was brick veneered and the Educational annex was erected in 1929 and 1930, these were removed for the present choir loft & baptistry.

In 1916, the pipe organ was installed; in 1965, the baptistry was renovated and a memorial window was installed. In 1965, a church library was organized; and in 1968, the Stigler Building located at the rear of the property was replaced with an education annex.

FIRST PRESBYTERIAN CHURCH (PCA)

The Lexington Presbyterian Church was organized May 1, 1834, with twelve charter members. Samuel Long, husband of Felice Leflore and brother-in-law of Greenwood Leflore, donated the lot for the original church building.

During the pastorate of Rev. J. B. Hutton a new sanctuary in the Gothic style with stained glass windows and bell tower was dedicated on June 17, 1894.

In 1911, a manse adjacent to the sanctuary was completed and used as such until fire damage it in 1968, at which time a new manse was purchased.

The damaged manse was renovated for use as an educational building and served as such until 1989 when replaced with the Allen Educational Building.

In 1924, the current sanctuary building was constructed, providing additional Sunday School rooms. It was renovated in 1975 with new stained glass windows, light fixtures, and an elevator. The downstairs Sunday School rooms were completely renovated in 2001.

On June 3, 1973, the congregation voted unanimously to ask the Presbytery of Central MS (PCUS) for dismissal to the Presbytery of the MS Valley (PCA). Permission was granted on July 19, 1973.

FIRST UNITED METHODIST CHURCH

On February 27, 1836, at a Quarterly Conference at Ebenezer Methodist Church, a building committee was appointed to build a church in Lexington, MS. In 1844, a one-room, frame building was constructed approximately three blocks from the current Church site. At this time, the church was a member of the Methodist Episcopal Church. In 1844 the church name was changed to Methodist Episcopal Church South.

On June 22, 1897, a building committee was appointed to construct a new church building on the current site; a new church was dedicated on March 6, 1898. In 1903, the Lexington church became a station church.

The current educational building annex was constructed in 1930 during the pastorate of Rev. J. E. Stevens. In 1939, the name of the church was changed to the Methodist Church. A parsonage was built on the original church site in 1941. In 1968, the church name was changed again to First United Methodist Church. The sanctuary was completely renovated in 1974.

ST. MARY'S EPISCOPAL CHURCH

St. Mary's Episcopal Church congregation was organized in the 1840s. On December 22, 1855, a church building was consecrated by priest-in-charge Benjamin Halstead on property called "Wanalaw" approximately 12 miles from the current church's location and was called Calvary Church. At that time, the congregation included seven families and twelve communicants. Services were held every Sunday at Calvary and also once a month in Lexington.

After a fire which totally destroyed the Calvary Church, its congregation diminished and that in Lexington increased. The decision was made to erect an Episcopal Church in St. Mary's Parish in Lexington. The new church was dedicated in 1880, and received a church bell in 1882 which continues to this day to summon worshipers to services.

In 1894, the church was completely destroyed by fire. But on March 11, 1900, a new St. Mary's Church was dedicated. In time, the bell was elevated and placed into a belfry over the front of the church. Later a vicarage was constructed adjacent to the church.

In 2000, the Parish House was remodeled and expanded to include office space and Sunday School rooms, and a sacristy was completed adjacent to the rear of the sanctuary.

ST. PAUL'S CHURCH OF GOD IN CHRIST

The Churches of God in Christ in the United States and foreign countries had their origin in Lexington, MS. The first organized Church of God in Christ congregation, St. Paul's and known as the "Mother Church," met in an abandoned gin house and was under the pastorate of Elder C. H. Mason, Sr. This gin house was located near the spot where the current church building stands today.

Rev. Mason organized the church in 1897 with the assistance of Rev. C. P. Jones and Rev. W. S. Pleasant and had a congregation of fifty to sixty organizing members. The first baptismal service was performed in March 1897.

The church began to grow beyond Lexington, and in 1907 to the First Assembly of the Church of God in Christ was formed in Memphis, TN.

The current pastor is Elder William Dean.

St. THOMAS CATHOLIC CHURCH

St. Thomas Catholic Church in Lexington is the only Catholic Church in Holmes County. In 1880, a Mission Church was organized for the many Irish Catholic peddlers who made Lexington their home.

Rev. M. F. Grignon served until 1879, at which time Father Lonergran took charge of Lexington as a mission and took steps to construct a permanent church structure,

The new church building was dedicated on April 24, 1887, for approximately one hundred communing parishioners. It grew to 172 at its peak.

In 1908, the original church and priest's house burned to the ground. The present church structure was built and dedicated in 1920, and a statue of the Blessed Virgin was given to the church by J. W. Conway. The present parish rectory was built in 1968. The first parish Council was established in March 1970, under the direction of Father Daniel Novak.

TEMPLE BETH-EL

In 1904, the Jewish citizens of Lexington formed a congregation. A lot was donated by Morris Lewis and Sam Herrman; and on that site, a temple was built.

On November 1, 1905, Temple Beth-El was dedicated. Mr. Henry Rosenthal was the first president of Temple Beth-El and was succeeded by Mr. Lewis. In 1906, a cemetery was established.

The congregation numbered 88 members at one point, and there were eighteen young men from the congregation who were in the service during World War II.

The Temple is affiliated with the Union of American Hebrew Congregations, and the Sisterhood is a member of the National Federation of Temple Sisterhoods.

The back side of the brochure indicated church tours were held Tuesday through Thursday and reservations were required. The guided tour includes a history of each church, an exterior tour, a limited interior tour, and a picnic lunch.

"A lot of visitors who come to Lexington are surprised to learn much of the town has been placed on the National Register of Historic Places," she said as he finished reading the brochure. She extended her hand and said, "We have two hundred and twenty-five contributing buildings on the National Register." She paused and smiled, "You are?"

"Jack Boulder. I'm here doing a little research for a client."

"I'm Susan," she said. "Genealogy research? The Courthouse is an excellent source for that. Just ask for Jean Ford-Smith, the Chancery Clerk. She can show you where all the records are located and can help you find anything you need."

Boulder nodded and said, "Have you worked here long?"

"About five years," she said. "I should say that I work here part time. I'm a volunteer."

"The man who just left said something about a boat?"

"He was talking about Blue Boy. It's a restored wooden yacht one of our local attorneys acquired and has on his farm."

"What's so special about this boat?"

"Briefly, the Blue Boy was built in nineteen twenty-eight at Long Beach, California, for the owner of the 7-Up Bottling Corporation. In nineteen thirty, it was confiscated by the Internal Revenue Service. Apparently it was being used to smuggle rum from Mexico up to Long Beach. The feds found hidden rum tanks under a false hull and chopped the boat up pretty good getting to those tanks. Within seven or eight months, William Randolph Hearst, apparently a friend of the original owner, bought the remains of Blue Boy and restored it to its former grandeur. He took it to the Pacific Coast Marina nearest to his San Simeon castle and kept it there for thirteen years. There it was known as the Little Yacht and was a favorite of Hearst's because he could operate it himself. He loved to take his movie star friends out for sunset cruises. Some of his artifacts are still on board, including a trophy he won in 1933 and a couple of photographs.

"In 1943, he donated the Blue Boy to the Navy which used it as a VIP tender for the Capital ships in Long Beach Harbor. After the war, the boat was sold to a Hollywood agent, and from there, it went through several Hollywood-type owners for several decades. Barbara Stanwyck once owned the boat, as did the greatest movie star of all time, Renaldo Duncan (the Cisco Kid).

"Probably the most famous story about the boat was that it was the vessel which President Kennedy took Marilyn Monroe on for a couple of 'rides.' On still nights one can sometimes detect just the faintest whisper of her voice, or so some people say."

Boulder considered this information and said, "Put me on the list to see that boat." He grinned and then scanned the office. "So, what is the Main Street Association? Is it the chamber of commerce?"

"It's the downtown development organization. We promote the downtown area primarily. As a matter of fact, we exist for the sole purpose of revitalizing Lexington's downtown and surrounding business district. We do that through something called the four-point approach." She held up a hand and raised a different finger as she counted off each point. "We do organization, economic development, design, and promotion of the district."

"I see," Boulder said.

"Lexington Main Street was organized in July two thousand and one with twenty-one board members representing all segments of the community. Since then we have won four Mississippi Main Street Association Downtown Revitalization Awards. We received the two thousand and four Best Small Town Image Promotion for the Lexington Main Street website, the two thousand and five Best Annual Fund-raiser for Taste Buds Men's Cooking Competition, the two thousand and five Best Image Promotion for the Lexington Promotional Brochure, and the two thousand and seven Merchant of the Year, who was Dayle Dillon Diffey of Peoples Drug Store."

"That's quite a drug store. I was in there just a few minutes ago."

"Now you know. Don't let the storefronts fool you. In Lexington, there's always the unexpected inside."

"That sounds like a commercial."

"In truth, I guess it is," she said with a soft laugh. "But it's the truth."

"Anything I shouldn't miss while I'm in Lexington?"

"Well, speaking of the unexpected. If you have a moment, while you are at the Courthouse ask Earline Wright Hart, the Circuit Clerk, to show you the mural in the basement of the Courthouse."

"What will I see?"

"I'm not telling," she said with a smile. "You will just have to see for yourself."

"The basement of the Courthouse," Boulder said. "Thanks for the information."

CHAPTER 18

Boulder walked back to the sheriff's office and asked to see Chief Deputy Adams. He was told Adams would be out in a few minutes. Boulder waited in the small reception room until Adams appeared. They went back to the conference room

"It didn't take long for the information on the Glock to come back," Adams said, laying a file jacket on the table. "We got a hit on it right away. Reported stolen from the trunk of a police officer's car. He's from South Carolina and was passing through Mississippi on his way to Dallas. He and his wife were staying at a motel just outside of Jackson."

"How long ago?" Boulder asked.

Adams referred to a piece of paper in the file. "Three weeks ago."

"And who is the driver of my Camaro?"

"That would be one Jimmy DeSoto of Jackson, Mississippi. He's got a rap sheet a mile long."

"What did he say about the gun?" Boulder asked.

"I'll let you read it for yourself, but I'll deny it if you ever say you saw this." Adams slid two typewritten pages in front of Boulder. It was the statement of Jimmy DeSoto. In part, it read:

> "... Rico and I were in Lexington on October 31 for the purpose of obtaining a Mustang for Mr. Richard Perry, who sends us orders for certain types of cars. He acquires vehicles for Mr. Greene, who lives in Chicago. I had heard from a relative that a woman in Lexington had a new Mustang. We came to Lexington to obtain the Mustang. I observed

Rico shoot the driver, who was an older woman, while he was taking the Mustang. I was close by in another car. I did not know Rico had a gun or how it got into the car I was driving today..."

"So he says Rico pulled the trigger on Mildred Monroe," Boulder said.

"I wouldn't believe that for a minute," Adams said. "Rico will say DeSoto did it. But notice who he says he was stealing the cars for."

"Richard Perry," Boulder noted. "Why does that name sound familiar?"

"You said you were followed on the way up, and you gave me a tag number to run a twenty-eight on. That's who it came back as being registered to. This may be just what we need to put Mr. Perry where he belongs."

"And what about this Mr. Greene who lives in Chicago? You don't think that could be Gregory Greene, do you?"

"I doubt it," Adams replied. "Our Gregory Greene is a TV weatherman—a high profile position."

"Thanks, Chief. You've been a great help. I appreciate it." They stood up and shook hands. "Oh, are you finished with my car?"

"I don't know of any reason we need it anymore. I'll get you a form you need to give to the tow truck company. If you find anything of interest that wasn't there when you last had possession of it, please let me know."

"I will," Boulder assured him. He got the form and headed to where his Camaro had been towed.

CHAPTER 19

Washington Wrecker Service was located on the outskirts of town in what a real estate broker might describe as not exactly being in the growth pattern. Old mobile homes and even older ramshackle houses littered the landscape. For Hubert Washington this was just fine. It gave his junk-car lot plenty of room to expand without in-town residents protesting too much. Some would describe his three businesses as necessary evils, but to Washington his auto repair shop, the junk auto parts business and the towing service provided a man such as him a way to make a pretty good living in a rural Mississippi county with only 21,148 residents, according to the latest census estimates.

Hubert Washington was forty-two years old, an avid reader of Western novels, a bream fisherman and husband of nine years to the former Estelle Clarke, a woman who had four children under the age of twelve when she and Washington got married. Hubert and Estelle had no children of their own though it was not for lack of trying. They assumed it was Hubert's problem, but it never became an issue. The way Hubert figured it, he had married a ready-made family. The children, three girls and a boy, adored him, so what was the point of having biological children? Their father was a deadbeat who got killed by a shot from a derringer after an argument in a card game when the oldest kid was ten years old. The man had never been around anyway, so it was natural that the kids saw Hubert as their father. Hubert Washington's enterprises provided ample support for the family, and they all lived out in the country in a nice little brick house surrounded by ten acres of rolling land. For Hubert Washington, life was good and nothing was going to spoil it. Every day, including Sunday when his family went to First Baptist Church, he wore a black cowboy hat and black boots. During the week he wore an identical hat and boots, only dirtier. He played it safe, kept his mouth shut and worked hard.

Because of his nature, Washington was suspicious when a man pulled up in front of his shop late that morning and asked to look at a vehicle his tow truck driver had towed in yesterday. He was even more uncomfortable when the man produced a business card reading, "Jack Boulder, Private Investigator." Nevertheless, Washington was a man who cooperated and who knew how to stay out of trouble. After all, the FBI had visited his lot once and recovered a stolen car that had been abandoned and towed to the Washington Wrecker yard at the request of the Highway Patrol.

"I understand your company towed in a sixty-eight Camaro yesterday?" Jack Boulder asked.

"That's right," Washington said. "It's inside the repair shop. The driver said it could not be released without police authorization."

"I believe this is the form you need," Boulder said, handing him an official release document from the Holmes County Sheriff's Department.

"That's it," Washington said. "Come on inside and let's take a look at it."

Their inspection revealed the car was drivable, although some body work and repair on the front suspension was necessary to put it back exactly in the shape it had been. Upon Boulder's inquiry, Washington assured him the work could be done right here in the shop.

"You don't know how good it is to see that car," Boulder said.

"I heard that," Washington said in amplified Southern drawl. "Do you drive it as your everyday car?"

"I drive it around Jackson when I need to, but I almost always rent a car when I go out of town."

"The Christmas parade is coming up this Saturday in Lexington. They usually have it on the first Thursday evening in December, but they thought they would try something different this year. There will be a section of the parade with antique cars in it. Quite a few people around here have antique cars and muscle cars like this one. I'm sure they would love to have you drive this one in the parade. We can have it ready for you Saturday morning."

"That would be something I've never done."

"Hold on," Washington said. "Let me get the name of the person to call."

Boulder considered the idea. The more he thought about it, the more he liked it. He visualized himself and Laura driving around the Lexington Square in the Camaro.

CHAPTER 20

Boulder got in the rental car and headed back to Jackson on Highway 17. About a mile prior to the interstate he noticed a distinctive, two-story brick building on the right side of the road. It reminded him of the type of early American building style one would see in Virginia. One of those official state historical markers stood at attention on the shoulder of the road. Curiosity got the best of him, so he pulled over and read the marker as twilight approached.

> **O.E.S. BIRTHPLACE**
> Here in 1849 Robert Morris, Mason, Schoolmaster, began movement that resulted in creation of the Order of the Eastern Star. Schoolhouse has also housed Masons and Co. C 15th Miss. Inf., C.S.A.

What was so familiar about this? He had heard of the Masons, and the Eastern Star name made a vague ring of a bell. He turned and noticed a small weatherproof box attached to the chain length fence where it met the gate. He opened the container and found a stack of brochures. He removed one, went back to the car and learned about the Little Red Schoolhouse and the...

> Order of the Eastern Star. The cornerstone of the building was laid in 1847. The original name was Richland Literary Institute, but in the mid-1800s was chartered under the name of Eureka Masonic College. In 1959, the Holmes County Board of Supervisors leased the property to the Order or the Eastern Star, Grand Chapter of Mississippi. Restoration of the building continued until 1979. In August of each year, a Festal Day picnic that attracts hundreds of Eastern Star families is held on the grounds. The degree

called Eastern Star was established by Dr. Robert Morris, Poet Laureate for Masonry, for women who subscribed to the ideals of Masonry. In Jackson, Mississippi, a marker in Smith Park commemorates the spot where the degrees of Eastern Star were first conferred.

Still, there was something more familiar about this, and it was not exactly that déjà vu feeling so common to most people. What was it about the Little Red Schoolhouse? Then it hit him. This was where Chief Deputy Adams told him the suspect's car had crashed after the chase on Halloween night. He got out and walked along the chain-link fence in moist, ankle-high grass, scanning the ground as he did so. At the end of the fence, he discovered two ruts in the ground leading from the roadway to the fence. He saw that the soil under a large oak tree at the end of the fence appeared to have been disturbed. Scouring the ground, he saw shards of red-plastic automobile tail-light lenses and assorted pieces of chrome and glass. At a spot just past the oak tree, he noticed something black and shaped like a small book. He walked to it, reached down and picked up the wet, leather-bound article. He turned back the cover and saw that it was a planner/organizer. On the title page was the name "Mildred Monroe," underneath which was a space titled, "in case of emergency" and under that was the contact information for Reverend Robert Lauderdale. The pages were saturated together but could still be turned and read individually if caution was used. The ink had spread, but the entries were readable. He turned the pages slowly and delicately. There were only a few appointments, most of the pages being notes about errands to do, meetings to attend or calls to make. It was not the calendar of a business executive or a busy professional. There were many days when there were no entries. He turned to October 31. At the bottom of the page was the entry, "Saint Paul's tonight." On the next page was an entry, "send flowers to Richardson family," and "pay bills." Boulder decided to take the calendar home with him and try to dry it out, lest he destroy any of the wet pages. Before leaving, he scanned the area for other items that might have been ejected from the car. Seeing nothing of interest, he got in his rental car and drove back to Jackson.

Back at his condo, he used a hair dryer to blow around the edges of the calendar without hitting the pages directly and tearing them out. It was slow going. So slow, he decided to try another method. He spotted a floor vent where his heated air came out. He laid the calendar on the vent and then checked his email and voice messages. There was nothing of major urgency or significance.

He went back to the calendar, which had dried somewhat, and peeled it open to October 31. He slowly turned each page backward through the year. Nothing caught his eye until October 10, when there was a notation, "Jackson to Chicago, Southwest," two flight numbers and "Gwen will pick up." He went to his computer and checked the Southwest Air Lines schedule to Chicago. Sure enough, the flight numbers matched. There was a weekly mid-morning flight direct to Chicago's Midway Airport and an early evening flight from Chicago to Jackson.

Did Mildred Monroe go to Chicago three weeks before her death to meet with Gregory Greene? If this calendar was accurate, the answer was right in front of him. And if this was the answer, it raised more questions, not the least of which was why his client did not tell him about the visit, and why Dr. Gwendolyn Warren did not say anything about it. He got the distinct impression from his interview with Gwen Warren that her relationship with Mildred Monroe was close, but not that close. He thought back on the interview with her and realized that although she had answered every question he had asked her, she was not exactly an overflowing fountain of information. Yes, he had more questions. And he suspected the answers might be found in Chicago. He glanced at his wristwatch. It was now almost 9:30 p.m. Chicago would have to wait until tomorrow.

CHAPTER 21

"Line one is for you, Lieutenant. Some guy from Mississippi named Jack Boulder. He said you would know the name."

Lieutenant Jerry Jasper, commander of a special detachment of the Organized Crime Division of the Chicago Police Department, not only knew Jack Boulder's name, he practically worshiped Jack Boulder, the man who had once saved his life during a hostage standoff. Jasper was in St. Louis working on a joint organized crime operation with the Chicago P.D., the FBI and the St. Louis P.D. During a stakeout, he was captured by the subjects of the stakeout after he walked into the wrong room unexpectedly. During an intense standoff, one of Jasper's captors "negotiated" an escape by agreeing to walk through the police barricade with a gun held to Jasper's head. Jasper had become the hostage. As hostage-taker and hostage walked by, Boulder raised his gun quickly and shot the subject in the head. It all looked so easy and simple in retrospect, but the real danger was in letting the captor leave the scene with the hostage. Jasper knew that if Boulder had not done what he had done when he did it, the subject would have executed him. After it was over, Jasper told Boulder if there was ever anything Lieutenant Jerry Jasper could do for him in Chicago to please call. Jasper hoped he could begin to repay the man who had saved his life. He poured his fourth cup of coffee and checked the big clock on the wall. It was 9:00 a.m.

"Jack Boulder," Jasper said. "It's good to hear from you. How can I help you?"

"You too," Boulder said. "How's the family?"

"Just great," Jasper lied. The family was not well at all. After the shooting, Jasper' wife feared he had come too close to being one of the fifty or so police officers who are killed in the line of duty each year in the United States. She wanted to have children, and she wanted those children have a father who would be reliable and would be there for them. She urged him to consider other employment. She even enlisted the support of his mother. Mother and wife ganged up on him verbally, constantly asking him when he was going to retire. Fortunately, there were no children. Finally, the day came when a suburban Chicago police officer was wounded in the line of duty. Jasper's wife gave him an ultimatum: "You can have the career in law enforcement or you can have me." He did not know how to tell her the truth. Should he lie to her and say he really wanted a law enforcement career, but he loved her more than anything? Or should he just quit and live the rest of his life in misery? He thought of other police officers who had left law enforcement in similar circumstances, all of whom had come back around the station house and said they had regretted the decision. His indecision was all his wife needed. She left him and wished him luck. The divorce was final six months later. He threw himself into his work and an occasional bottle of bourbon.

"Have you ever heard of a guy named Gregory Greene?" Boulder asked.

"Would that be the same Gregory Greene that does the television weather here in the Windy City?"

"That would be the one."

"Let me call you back on a secure line," Jasper said. Within seconds, Boulder's telephone rang. "You really hit a home run, Jack. We've been interested in Greene quite a bit lately. In addition to his celebrity gig on the television, he owns several suspicious businesses in town. He's got an auto dealership, a music store and a restaurant. They have always been marginal from what we can tell. We're looking into his involvement in a counterfeiting operation distributing counterfeit CD's and DVD's. There are two areas we're mostly concentrating on right now. The first is a money laundering operation involving the restaurant. It seems his little blue-plate restaurant is reporting sales in excess of fifty-thousand a week to the tax officials. We're also looking hard at his automobile dealership. We have good reason to believe there is an interstate car-theft ring operating out of the body shop. It seems he specializes in filling orders for high-income customers in other countries."

"Tell me more about the stolen car ring," Boulder said. "We seem to have a problem with that here in Mississippi."

"We believe the vehicles are stolen by local car thieves in U.S. cities and then smuggled to waiting ships at ports in New Orleans, Miami, and Houston, among other cities. We think Greene's people are coordinating the thefts. Sometimes the vehicles come to his body shop in Chicago. Sometimes they are shipped to black-market dealers all over the world, including places like the Middle East where foreign militants fighting in Iraq are thought to be bringing them in from countries across the region. We have one case in which several sport utility vehicles were stolen and turned up in the Middle East. The feds believe they were going to be used in car bombings. What's been going on in Mississippi?"

"I'm familiar with two cases you might be interested in. The first involves my personal car." Boulder related the events surrounding his Camaro. "The second case was a carjacking of an almost new Mustang. Unfortunately, the driver was shot and killed in the carjacking. The driver of the stolen car was arrested, but he's clammed up and won't say a thing. We think we may have the shooter. We recovered the gun."

"The M.O. with your Camaro is being used all over the country right now," Jasper said. "A wrecker pulls up to a broke-down motorist and tows the vehicle away. They have figured out a way to disarm the GPS too. These are not amateurs."

"You might also be interested in knowing the owner of that Mustang—the one who was killed—was Greene's high school English teacher."

"Now that's a mighty bit of a coincidence." Jasper said.

"That's what I thought, and that's why I'm calling. I found the victim's calendar and there are entries indicating she flew to Chicago on October 10 to meet with Gregory Greene."

"Hold on," Jasper said. After a short pause, Jasper was back. "We had him under surveillance on October tenth. Can you give me a description of the victim?"

"Female, African-American, mid-sixties," Boulder replied.

"Got it right here. He did his noon weather show at the television station. Afterwards, he met such a person in his apartment on East Huron Street at approximately one thirty p.m. She met him in the lobby and they got on an elevator together. She came back down alone an hour later and then got in a taxi. He came down fifteen minutes later and was chauffeured back to the television station."

"Interesting," Boulder said. "That is very useful. I'll be back in touch."

CHAPTER 22

The December weather outside was cold and windy, but inside the cavernous tennis center, the temperature was a balmy seventy-two degrees. Barbara Calhoun bounced the fuzzy, yellow tennis ball firmly on the hard court at her feet and then tossed it in the air, remembering what her fifty-dollar-an-hour tennis pro instructor had told her. "Toss it straight up so it would land on the base line if it fell." The toss was perfect, and Barbara's racquet arched up and then forward, sending the ball over the top of the net by an inch and into the receiver's box straight for her opponent, another woman in her fifties in the Metro Ladies Tennis Association. The ball hit the frame of the player's racquet on the other side of the net and bounced out of bounds.

"Good serve," she said, which is tennis lingo for "Damn it, I should have been able to return that."

Barbara moved to the left side of the court to serve to the other opposing player. This was a doubles match, and a very important one. The team winning this match would advance to the State Championships. Winning that tournament would mean a trip to the Southern Region Championships. Barbara's team of twelve was a collection of the best over-fifty women's tennis players in the Jackson area. It had won the state championship the past two years in a row, but had placed no higher than third in the Southern Regionals. This was going to be the year they would win there. What made this year's team much better was the addition of Jewel Grenada, a former college tennis player who had just this year become eligible to play on a seniors' team by virtue of turning age fifty. Every seniors' team in three counties had recruited her in ways only women can. Grenada wound up choosing Barbara's team for a simple reason—she was convinced Barbara's team had the best chance of advancing. All one need do was to just look at the record of the past three years.

Barbara executed another good toss and serve. The ball came back across the net to Barbara's partner who promptly smashed it between the two opposing players. Two more especially good serves and the game score stood at 5-4. Barbara and her partner would need only to win one more game, and they would win their match 6-4, 6-4. Their opponents had given them a tough match, but Barbara knew her side of the net would prevail. She had been in these situations many times before, and she sensed that momentum was on their side.

As the players changed sides of the court, they paused for a drink of water, a wipe from a wet towel and brief, shallow conversation. On the court next to them the match had just ended, and the four players there were shaking hands at the net. As they finished the ritual, Barbara motioned for one of the players on her team.

"How did you do?" Barbara asked.

"We won," came the smiling reply.

"Great!" Barbara said.

"But Peggy and Lois lost, so it's now up to you two. How are you doing?"

"We're up five to four in the second set. We won the first set."

"We'll be cheering for you."

Barbara walked back onto the court and got into position to receive the serve. So the whole season boils down to this. We win this game and we go to state. We lose and we stay home. We have to win only this next game. They must win three to win this set. State championships, here we come. I wish Clarence could be here to see this. All at once a strange feeling came over. Clarence had died just when she needed him most. Was she mad or sad? Whatever she was, she needed to get her mind back on the game.

Barbara's mind was still calculating the possibility of going to state when the serve came at her. She reacted with a too strong forehand, and the ball sailed far out of bounds on the other end of the court. Barbara's partner must have been similarly distracted because it took only four serves for the other team to win the game, making the score now 5-5. Barbara's partner, Leah, prepared to serve and told Barbara to take any balls at the net that she could get. Leah served and Barbara jumped to her left to attack the low return, but smacked it hard into the net. Barbara cursed under her breath and said meekly, "Good shot," which really meant, "Damn it. I should have had that one." The second point was even worse. Barbara lunged at the ball, which clipped her racquet and flew out across the court to her left. The third and fourth points were also lost, and suddenly Barbara and Leah found themselves on the losing side of a 6-5 score with their team watching them from the clubhouse deck only three courts away. Somebody yelled, "Come on girls, you can do it."

Unfortunately, Barbara and Leah failed to rise to the occasion and lost the next game, sending the match into a third set tiebreaker. Under the current league rules of tennis, instead of playing a full third set, when one team won the first set and the other won the second set, there was to be a ten-point tiebreaker, meaning the first team to score ten points by being at least two points ahead would win the third set, and therefore the match.

The third set tiebreaker began with Barbara and Leah winning the first point and then proceeded with long points in which each team played as if the state championship was on the line. Finally, it came down to a 9-9 tie score. This was the tennis version of sudden death. The next team to be ahead by two points would win the match. The next point went on longer than normal, each player being careful just to get it back across the net. Play safe tennis and let the opponent make the mistake. The strategy worked for their opponents as Leah hit the ball wide right while trying to hit a winning shot. Now Barbara would serve again.

Barbara called the score, "Nine–ten." Her toss was perfect as it had been all day, but she hesitated slightly and let the ball drop farther than normal before she swung. The result was a low shot right into the net. Her second serve must be perfect or they would lose. No problem. She had been here before. She made the toss and firmly, but carefully smacked the ball across the net deep into the receiver's box close to the line.

"Out," shouted the receiver.

For an instant, everyone stood still. Then the opponent who had not received the serve jumped up and yelled in delight. She grabbed her partner and the two of them started bouncing up and down like two high school cheerleaders on a trampoline.

"What?" Barbara said, with an edge in her voice. "That ball was not out." She pointed at the receiver's partner. "How did YOU see it?"

The player raised her hands as if to say, "Don't ask me." "I really couldn't tell," she replied. But Barbara could tell by the tone of her voice, she knew the ball had been in.

"What do you mean—you couldn't tell?! You've been calling my serves all day, and suddenly you can't tell. That was a slow, second serve. You saw it, and you know it was in."

"I don't know what to say," the other player replied.

Tennis etiquette demands the players shake hands at the net at the conclusion of the match. Leah stepped forward and held out her hand to the opponents, who stepped forward and shook hers in return.

Barbara yelled, "Nooooo!," in anguish and then smashed her racquet on the court with such force, the frame broke in two places. She left it on the court and stomped away. Her team members, Leah and the opposing team members stared in disbelief, their mouths open. They watched Barbara disappear toward the parking lot and heard the sound of screeching tires from her Mercedes convertible as she roared away.

Dick Alcorn, the regular letter carrier, walked up the circular driveway to the front door of the Calhoun residence, a five-thousand-square-foot, Mediterranean-inspired villa with a red, clay-tiled roof in the fashionable Eastover neighborhood of northeast Jackson. Bordered on each side by beveled-glass, the door had a mail slot in its middle at belt height. Although it would have been less convenient for him, Alcorn wished more people had letter slots in their doors instead of mailboxes on the street. Mailboxes were easier targets for theft and there had been several cases recently where someone had stolen statements from mailboxes and made thousands of dollars of purchases on the Internet before being caught. He had stayed after work twice in the past three weeks being interviewed by Postal Inspectors, one of whom seemed to imply Alcorn might have been in on some type of scam.

Alcorn slid the handful of envelopes into the slot. The letter carrier knew what would happen next. There was an immediate thump against the other side of door. The envelopes were snatched instantly by the Calhoun's cocker spaniel. Alcorn saw this phenomenon often. Why so many dogs were compelled to attack mail as it slid through the slots, he did not know. Most of the time, the dogs barked and growled, but the Calhoun dog was a quiet attacker. Alcorn hoped there was nothing in today's mail that would suffer damage caused by cocker spaniel teeth marks. He did not need a meeting with his supervisor about a customer complaint.

From the large, professionally-designed kitchen at the rear of the house, Barbara heard the noise of mail and dog. She walked resolutely to the front door, still smarting from the loss on the tennis court. She squatted and collected the scattering of white envelopes. She flipped through them. Nothing but bills. Then there was a knock on the door. She opened it immediately assuming it was the letter carrier. Instead, there stood a man she had never seen before.

"Mrs. Calhoun?"

"Yes."

"My name is Jack Boulder. May I speak with you about your contribution to the Save Our Saints organization? I believe you received a letter from Lexington?"

She looked puzzled, and then spoke. "Oh yes, I remember. Please come in. And forgive my appearance. I just came off the tennis court."

"No problem at all."

"Wait," she said. "Do you mind if I take a quick shower?"

"Uh, of course not," Boulder said.

"Make yourself at home and I'll be right back." She waved him toward an adjacent room and then headed up the stairs.

Boulder ambled in to what he would have called a small art museum. There was original artwork all over the walls. Too much of it, he thought. The floors in the place were either polished stone or some kind of fancy tile. The living room ceiling must have been fifteen feet tall, and the chandelier hanging from it was the gaudiest thing he had ever seen. A wide opening led to a second, more casual room displaying French doors opening to a botanical garden. Light streamed in through the clear glass panes. At one end of the room was a huge fireplace above which resided a mantel of porcelain figurines. Above that were even more paintings. In the middle of the room was a large table upon which a large vase of fresh flowers was displayed. He had never been to Italy, but he felt like this was a replica of some Italian place. It darn sure did not feel like Mississippi. The house was only one of five in the name of Mr. and Mrs. Clarence Calhoun. The others homes were in Vail, the Kensington section of London, the artsy Montrose section of Houston and a downtown apartment in Paris. The Paris residence on centrally-located Ile Saint-Louis was Barbara Calhoun's favorite.

Ten minutes later, Boulder heard a whisking sound behind him and turned to see Barbara Calhoun. If he were writing a description in a police report, it would have read: white female, approximately fifty-five years of age, green eyes, light brown hair, one hundred and fifteen pounds, five feet six inches, no identifying marks, last seen wearing a satiny navy blue jogging suit.

"How may I help you, Mr. Boulder?"

"I'm a private investigator. My client has asked me to find out who sent letters from Lexington to several people. Your name was on a list of addressees in the letter. The letter would have been from Mildred Monroe, thanking you for a contribution to Saints Academy in Lexington. I just wanted to verify you received the letter and ask if you had ever heard of Mildred Monroe."

"Yes. I've heard of Mildred Monroe. My husband said he would kill her if he thought he could get away with it."

CHAPTER 23

Barbara Calhoun cocked her head and gave Boulder a "So what did you think of that?" expression. Boulder looked down as though considering the unspoken question.

"Why would your husband say that?'

"She tried to blackmail him!"

"How so?"

Barbara Calhoun clasped her hands in front of her and said with a smile, "Could I get you something to drink, Mr. Boulder? I'm having a martini. We can go into Clarence's study. I believe the letter is there."

"Sure, why not?"

"Oh, good. Follow me." She led him back through the living room and then around a corner to an open door leading to the kitchen. "Just a moment," she said to Boulder and then in a louder voice to the kitchen, "Oh, Marilyn, please make two martinis and bring them to the study."

"Yes, mam," came a voice from somewhere deep in the kitchen area. Boulder thought it sounded like an older woman.

They continued the journey. He followed her through another open area and then down a hall into a dark-paneled, medium-sized room. On the walls were several stuffed deer heads, a wild boar head and a wild turkey. The place looked as much like a pub as anything else. Barbara Calhoun walked over to a bookcase where one of the shelves contained an eight-by-ten framed photograph of a small plane. She picked it up and displayed it to Boulder.

"This was my husband's pride and joy," she said. "He loved nothing more than to get in this plane, fly around the Delta, then land at the municipal airport. He would have somebody from the hunting camp pick him up and off they would go.

This time of year was his favorite. He was an avid deer hunter. He said the best deer hunting in Mississippi was in Holmes County."

She walked over to a large, mahogany desk and retrieved an envelope from a stack of papers.

"I think this is what you are looking for."

Boulder took it and removed the letter. It appeared to be identical to the one Gregory Greene had given him. The postmark was also from Lexington.

A plump woman in a white uniform dress entered the room. In her hands was a tray with two martinis. Barbara Calhoun instructed her to lay the tray on the desk. She did so and left the room. Calhoun picked up a drink in each hand and offered one to Boulder. There was no toasting. It was as if she was handing him a glass of water. She raised the martini glass to her mouth and drained half of it. Boulder took a polite sip from his glass.

"Do you know any of the other people the letter is addressed to?"

"No," she replied. "This was one of my husband's projects." Boulder gave her a quizzical look indicating he did not understand. She smiled a patronizing smile. "Clarence apparently made the commitment to contribute to the school for some period of time. I sent a check to that SOS organization the last week in October. I'm not sure I did the right thing. He died unexpectedly, and I'm trying to make certain his promises are kept. I think that is what he would have wanted me to do. You would do that, wouldn't you?"

"Of course," Boulder said. "Do you mind if I keep this letter?"

"Only if you will give me a copy in return," she said. "I'm serious about keeping proper records. You would not believe what people do to take advantage of widows."

"May I take it and make a copy? I'll bring the original back to you."

"You can just mail it," she said.

"You said your husband died unexpectedly?"

"He died in a helicopter crash in Italy in October."

"I'm sorry," Boulder said.

"They said he might have been flying the thing. He was sitting in the front with the pilot. It would not surprise me. I think he wished he could fly helicopters. He said that one day he was going to take lessons."

"You also said something to the effect that your husband said he would kill Mildred Monroe if he could get away with it?"

"She came here the week before he died. They met right here in this room. I could hear their voices were raised, but I couldn't tell what they were saying. I was in another part of the house and never even saw the woman. To this day, I've never seen the woman. After she left, I asked Clarence what all that was about. He said she had tried to extort some money from him. He said he had seen some desperate people in his time, but she took the cake. I thought she was some disgruntled employee from one of his businesses."

Boulder took a sip from the drink. The information was useful, but not immediately verifiable.

"Do you remember what kind of car she drove?"

"Her car?" She thought for a minute as she downed the last swallow of the martini. "I remember now. It was a red Mustang. One of those kinds that look like they did when I was in high school. I even had a red Mustang myself.

"Did your husband ever talk about Saints Academy?"

"Not to me, he didn't"

She walked him to the front door and Boulder bid her goodbye. He left with her letter. She went back to Clarence's office and finished off Boulder's martini.

CHAPTER 24

Boulder drove back to his condo, stopping on the way at a convenience store for a pair of polarized sunglasses. The weather for the past few days had been so gray, he forgot how bright the sun could be. Not finding any he liked on the rack, he made a mental note to stop in a drug store later in the day.

Back at his home office, he decided to do a quick Internet search of Clarence Calhoun. An international wire service carried the story of his death:

> MILLIONAIRE businessman Clarence Calhoun of Jackson Mississippi USA was killed when his helicopter crashed on a beach in the small resort village of Porto Ilia and burst into flames.
>
> Sunbathers and beach-goers watched in horror as the chopper plunged to the ground and tumbled across a beach in a ball of flame. Emergency services were jammed with witnesses calling on mobile phones.
>
> One of the emergency personnel said: "It was the worst aircraft crash I've ever seen. The debris just did not look like an aircraft—you couldn't recognize it.
>
> "The main body of the aircraft was still ablaze and there was quite a smell of fuel. Debris was spread over the beach for about 50 meters."
>
> The crash happened at about 1:30 p.m. yesterday. Reports are that the aircraft was a French-built, twin-engine Squirrel helicopter.
>
> Mr. Calhoun, 55, was not a qualified helicopter pilot, but was qualified to pilot small airplanes. There were reports

he was in the co-pilot seat. Fire crews used thermal imaging equipment to make sure no-one else was on board the four-seater helicopter. Police sealed off the area as crash investigators moved in. He had reportedly been in meetings in Naples earlier in the day.

Tributes poured in today in Mississippi for Mr. Calhoun, who had started in the oil exploration business with $93 (US) in his pocket.

Atlantic Rock Oil Corporation President Tyler Wayne said: "I am desperately sorry to learn of Clarence Calhoun's death. He was an outstanding man, a person who took an enormous interest in the well-being of the community in which he lived. He was a brilliant businessman who was extremely generous in his support for local initiatives. He will be enormously missed."

The rags to riches story of Mr. Calhoun began almost 30 years ago, when at the age of 22, he set up his company in a garage in Jackson, Mississippi USA.

The firm, which used state-of-the-art technology to find oil and gas, developed into a world leader. It was eventually sold in 1989 for $27 million.

A spokesperson for Mississippi Governor Eileen Kemper said: "Calhoun involved himself as a state business leader and a great philanthropist and he will be greatly missed."

In addition to his business dealings, Calhoun received notoriety in 1999 when he was accused of paying bribes to an advisor to the Governor of a Mexican state over an oil contract. The case was never prosecuted.

Boulder considered the information. The story was dated October 20. That meant he died on October 19 if the article was correct. It also meant he had been visited by Mildred Monroe the week prior to that. It was consistent with what Barbara Calhoun had said. It seemed she was not exactly grief-filled over her husband's death, but that was not his concern.

Barbara Calhoun's comments about hunting, and perhaps the hunting atmosphere in Clarence Calhoun's home office, aroused something in Boulder. He recalled his youth when hunting was an important part of growing up in Mississippi, even though he lived in the city. He remembered his first .22 rifle, his first .410 shotgun and his ultimate hunting weapon, a Remington 1100 shotgun. Was it the guns and the hunting, or was it just being out in the woods with nature that appealed to so many Mississippi boys? Perhaps it was the camaraderie of hunting with friends and fathers. Whatever it was, he felt the need to explore it some more.

He was so lost in his thoughts, he was pulling into his parking place at his condo before he knew. He barely remembered driving home. Inside, he sat down at his computer and checked the Lexington Main Street Association website. He clicked here and there for a few minutes and found a directory of members entitled "Outdoor Enthusiasts." Now, how many chambers of commerce had such a category? He studied the list and saw outfitters, hunting supply stores, a wildlife refuge, an ATV and hunting-gear dealership, guided hunt providers, federal and state agencies that issued licenses, a state park and even a wild game processing place. He clicked on one of the links and discovered he could stay in a private lodge and dine twice a day in a "cook-house" next to the lodge. The menu included everything from smoked deer roasts to smothered quail. All he needed to bring was his Mississippi hunting license, his gun with ammunition, warm camouflage clothing and hiking boots and casual clothing and toiletries. Deer and turkey hunts were available. He decided when this case was over, he would ask Chief Deputy "Rosey" Adams if he would like to go on a hunting trip.

The thought reminded him he should call the Chief Deputy. He called Adams' office number and told him he had made contact with Barbara Calhoun and had verified she had indeed received a letter identical to the one Greene received.

"And you were going to fax a copy of that letter to me," Adams said.

"Right. Sorry about that. What's your fax number again? I'll fax a copy of the letter to you immediately."

Adams gave him the fax number to the Holmes County Sheriff's Department. Boulder told him he needed to hang up so he could fax the document but would call back in a minute. He fed the document into the communications device and dialed Adams' number. He pressed the "send" button and waited until the telephonic squawking sounds had ended. He called Adams again and asked if he had received the fax.

"I've got it right here," Adams said. "Are you coming back here anytime soon?"

"Later today," Boulder said.

"Good, because I have something to tell you, but I can't tell you over the telephone. Come by the office. We're going to go for a little ride." Adams lowered his voice to a whisper. "I can't tell you inside this building."

"What's that?"

"I know who sent the letters."

CHAPTER 25

Jack Boulder felt fantastic as he approached the Square in Lexington. With a smile on his face, he turned off the radio and started whistling. The sun was bright (oh, yes, must get those sunglasses), the air was crisp and clear, a hunting trip was possible and he felt he was making progress on the case. The call from Adams had made his day. Obviously the Chief Deputy had seen something in the letter. Perhaps it was a way Mildred's name had been signed, or rather forged. Maybe it was a phrase used often by a certain person. Once, Boulder had a case where someone always drew a certain type of little round happy face just below her name. When Boulder showed it on a letter to someone who saw the happy face on a regular basis, the identity was immediate. What was it that made Adams know who it was? Whatever it was, he was now anxious to find out.

The Holmes County Courthouse looked radiant in the bright sun. Its unique clock tower reaching skyward as it harkened the way to the center of town. As Boulder drove around the Courthouse, he heard a siren and looked ahead to see an ambulance entering the Square. With red lights flashing and siren yelping, it negotiated the busy area and headed south. It reminded Boulder of the beginning of the chase of his Camaro. Yes, this is going to be a good day.

He parked and went inside the sheriff's office. As he did so he heard screaming and the commotion of someone going berserk. These are not uncommon sounds in police stations or sheriff's offices. Visitors get upset when they see friends or family members incarcerated. Sometimes fights break out among people who have found themselves in trouble with the law. One of the more dangerous times in law enforcement work is the moment handcuffs are removed from a prisoner. Boulder had seen more than one seemingly docile prisoner go into a fit of rage when the handcuffs came off. His body tensed as he got ready to grab a fleeing prisoner or assist with a violent one.

The screams were coming from the dispatcher. She was flailing against a wall yelling, "No, no, no." A male deputy was behind her, his arms around her waist holding her like a rodeo cowboy holds a calf he is attempting to rope. She lashed out from side to side and struck her head on the side of a file cabinet. Her blood splattered against the wall. The officer holding her yelled out, "I need some help in here." Boulder lunged toward them and pushed them toward a corner, blood now on Boulder's shirt and arm. Now pushed into the corner, her body slowed down. Her yells turned to groans as if she had a horrible abdominal pain.

"It's okay now," Boulder said. "We are here for you. Just settle down."

His words incited her. She started yelling and bucking again as the two men held on and pushed toward the corner.

"There, there," Boulder said, as soothingly as possible. She was still all of a sudden, as if she had given in to the demon possessing her. The three of them stood there arm in arm. Boulder noticed the male officer was crying also.

"What happened?" Boulder asked.

"Rosey's dead," she sobbed. "Rosey's dead."

CHAPTER 26

Roosevelt "Rosey" Adams was dead on arrival at University Hospital & Clinics. The news spread like wildfire in the small town. WXTN and WAGR radio stations interrupted programming with the news. Within two hours, flowers were being delivered to the Holmes County Sheriff's Department with no instructions except "In memory of Rosey." Lexington florists ran out of roses because of so many orders. The excitement of spreading the message quickly turned into shock for many citizens. Soon Rosey's body would be taken to Porter & Sons' Funeral Home.

Jack Boulder went to a restaurant and sipped coffee for thirty minutes. He never looked up. He finally got up and went to the Courthouse. He recalled someone had told him to check out the basement. He needed something to do. A lady in the Circuit Clerk's office led him down a stairwell to a single room.

"What's the story on this room?" Boulder asked.

"It used to be the holding cell," she said. "That's why the commode is in there. Anyway, this man came and did murals on all the walls to commemorate the history of the Church of God in Christ. It started in Lexington, you know."

She left and Boulder scanned the low-ceilinged room. It could not have been more than eight-feet by six-feet. Sure enough, there was a mural on every wall. There was also a story printed out on heavy paper above each mural. The colors were brilliant. One of the papers provided an introduction and the name of the artist:

> From the gin house to Mason Temple a pioneering path was made. Someone said "a picture is worth a thousand words." May these illustrations of Bishop Mason in art help to commemorate his memory and legacy.
>
> The artist Eld. Samuel Foster Greenville, MS
> September, 1997.

Boulder read some of the panels.

MASON TEMPLE
The COGIC'S history is a great legacy. The COGIC grew rapidly from the first gin house. Churches sprung up in cities in every state of the United States. Mason Temple, the church's headquarters was built and is located in Memphis, Tenn. Many great worship services and historical moments have taken place there. The last and great "I've been to the mountaintop" speech of Dr. M. L. King was delivered in Mason Temple. The temple was recently visited by the president of the United States, President Bill Clinton. Bishop Mason's life ended in 1961. He is entombed on Mason Temple grounds. His epitaph reads, "God will not forget your labors of love ye have administered to the Saints."

THE FIRST CHURCH OF GOD IN CHRIST
The first Church of God in Christ building was a small old cotton gin house located on the bank of a creek in

Lexington, Mississippi. People from surrounding areas were drawn there to hear the doctrines of holiness Bishop Mason preached.

ARREST
Bishop Mason did not escape persecution and trial. His service was shot into while they were praising God by an evil affected person. No one was killed but this did not hinder the great success of the church. It grew even more. Bishop Mason was arrested in Holmes County while doing work for the Lord. He was a Holy man, one of great integrity, he went quietly with the officer to jail.

THE JAIL EXPERIENCE
Just as Saint Paul spent time in jail, it befell also our Founding Leader, Bishop C.H. Mason. While in jail, he prayed with the Lord who heard and delivered him, and was with him throughout his troubles and trials.

A PRAYER IN THE WOODS
Bishop Mason was a man of much prayer. As our Lord would often spend time out alone in prayer on the hillsides, to be strengthened in power and instructed of God, so did our Founding Leader pray much. With the responsibility as chief apostle of COGIC, he would often resort to the Lord in prayer for guidance for his great church. There was a time in his early ministry when he went into the woods to pray and while there received guidance from the Lord. Bishop Mason would often quote I Timothy 2:1-6: "I exhort therefore, that, first of all, supplications, prayers, intercessions, and giving of thanks be made for all men; for kings, and for all that are in authority; that we may lead a quiet and peaceful life in all godliness and honesty. For this is good and acceptable in the sight of God our Saviour..."

The room added perspective to his mood. All of us will leave this earth. It is our works that remain.

He drove back to Jackson.

CHAPTER 27

If Save Our Saints was a foundation, then surely it must be registered somewhere. Federal? State? Local? He did not know where, but he knew who would know. He called Laura at her office.

"A quick legal question," he said. "I know you're busy."

"Never too busy for you. Whatcha got?"

"I'm working on a case involving a foundation, or a charity, or whatever they call it. The thing is called Save Our Saints, and it's supposed to be set up to raise money for a school."

"Are you at home?"

"Yes," he said, and walked to the French doors of his condominium. He looked across Smith Park and up to an upper floor of the tall downtown office building where Laura's law offices were located. Although the windows in the building were smoke black he could see her silhouette. He raised his phone as if tipping a glass in salute.

"There is a woman named Julia Youngblood, who interned with our firm while she was in law school. She now works in the Secretary of State's Office. Just go to the receptionist and ask for her. She knows everything there is to know about foundations, nonprofit organizations and charities in Mississippi."

"Thanks. I'm on the way."

"Be sure to tell her I said hello," Laura said.

"I'll do that. Are we still on for dinner?"

"Look for me at your front door at seven" she said. "And I am already hungry for your spaghetti and a good cabernet."

In his mind he could see her winking. As they said good-bye he made a mental note to make a trip to the liquor store.

Boulder snatched a jacket and note pad and trooped the block and a half to the headquarters building of the Mississippi Secretary of State. Five minutes later, he was seated across from a massive wood desk upon which was perched a nameplate reading "Julia Youngblood," and behind which sat a woman of approximately fifty years of age wearing a navy blue suit and white blouse. Her hair was black with streaks of gray. A wall of law books and a credenza were behind her. She looked "official" all the way. Hardly what Boulder had expected when Laura used the words "intern" and "law student."

"Laura Webster told me to tell you hello," Boulder said.

"And likewise to her from me," she said. "She has mentioned you several times. You must be working on a case?"

"Yes. I need some information about nonprofit organizations. One in particular called Save Our Saints. It's up in Lexington."

"Hold on," she said. She picked up the telephone, punched it a few times and said, "Would you bring me the file on Save Our Saints?"

Suddenly, Boulder noticed there was no computer in the office. It had been a while since he had been in an office where there was not a computer at hand. She read his mind.

"I suppose you are wondering why I don't have a computer."

"Well, I..."

"They tell me I have what is known as logizomechano-phobia, or the fear of computers," she said. "I know it is an irrational thing, and I am working on it."

"Good for you," Boulder said. "It must have been tough getting through law school."

"Almost did not make it. Fortunately, I have a high school daughter who helped me."

"When did you graduate?"

"This past May," she said.

"Pardon my getting personal, but..."

"I know... What's a middle-aged woman like me doing going to law school? It was a matter of personal pride. Up until four years ago, I had always been involved in community organizations, philanthropy and volunteerism. Then my husband died unexpectedly. I needed to do something more with my life than give away money. I threw myself into studying law and the career I never had." Just then, a clerk came in and handed Julia Youngblood a file folder. "Anyway, enough about me. You're here about this nonprofit corporation." She opened the file folder and studied the documents for a moment. She looked up and said, "Do you have a computer and Internet access?"

"I do," Boulder replied.

"You can go online and get most of this information. But just looking at it, it appears everything is in order. We ask for the names of the individuals responsible for custody of funds, distribution of funds, individuals responsible for fund-raising, individuals responsible for custody of financial records, individuals authorized to sign checks and the bank in which registrant's funds are deposited. In this case, the individual was one Mildred Monroe." She looked up and raised an eyebrow as if asking if that was the expected name.

"That would be she," Boulder said.

"According to the application, the purpose of the organization is to raise funds for the support and continuation of Saints Academy in Lexington."

"Does it show how much has been raised?"

"It only shows the most recent annual statement. Not what the organization might have taken in during the current year."

She shuffled through the file. "Last year's statement showed an income of thirty thousand dollars."

"Does anything look out of the ordinary?"

"Not really."

"Is there a board of directors, or other people who might be involved listed anywhere?" Boulder asked.

"The board of the nonprofit is comprised of Mildred Monroe, Reverend Robert Lauderdale, Gwendolyn Warren, and Ruthie Mae Hinds. The agent for process is Gus Rankin, attorney."

"Any updates since October thirty-first?"

"Not that I see here," the state lawyer said. "What happened on October thirty-first?"

"That is the date she was killed."

"Oh, my goodness."

"You mentioned bank deposits. Does it show which bank they used?"

"That would be BankPlus in Lexington."

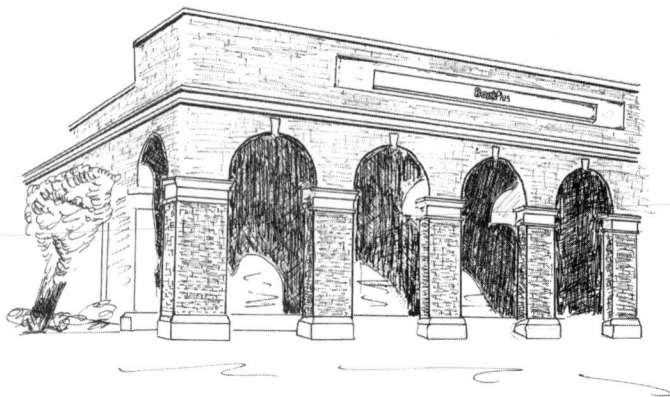

CHAPTER 28

Ruthie Mae Hinds turned to Dr. Gwendolyn Warren and said, "You think I have it now?"

"Yes, Miss Ruthie Mae," Gwen Warren said. "Just read it like it is. Be as natural as you can without sounding like you are reading."

They were sitting by the telephone in Ruthie Mae's living room. It was 5:15 p.m. Ruthie Mae was grateful for the visits she had received from Dr. Gwen Warren since the evening Mildred Monroe was shot in the parking lot at the church. A week afterwards, Ruthie Mae's nerves had gotten the best of her and she sought professional help. She was referred to a counselor in town, Dr. Gwendolyn Warren. Turned out Gwen was a former student of Mildred, Ruthie Mae's best friend in the entire world. Ruthie Mae and Mildred were the "old maids" of Lexington. Some said their lack of husbands was the only thing the two of them had in common. After all, Mildred was a free spirit who was young at heart and loved being around young people. Ruthie Mae had no use for kids, or men for that matter, and she was more of a homebody. She loved her garden and her books. She drew a decent retirement income from a federal government agency where she had been an accounting clerk in the nearby district office. She loved and admired Mildred. Truth is, she wished she could have been like Mildred. There was some peace in her heart that the last thing Mildred had attended was a birthday party Ruthie Mae had organized.

Ruthie Mae's visits to Dr. Gwen Warren had been very productive. Although reluctant to share her feelings at first, things got better with each visit. Dr. Warren had explained there were often many stages of grief, and it would take some time to go through each. The first stage was shock. In this stage, a person might feel numb, out of touch with reality and even like they are living in another world. The second stage was denial, which amounts to being unable to accept the situation. It is an attempt to avoid the inevitable. Next comes anger. This is the one Ruthie Mae had the most problem with. She was a pacifist if there ever was one. Nonviolence was in her blood. She had proven over and over in her life that she could withstand abuse without having to physically fight back. But now she wanted to kill. She felt she could push the button to electrocute whomever killed Mildred. It was a strange emotional time for her. She was not concerned so much that she wanted to seek revenge, but because it actually gave her pleasure to think of getting revenge. In the final stage of grieving, there would be resolution, but that would come for Ruthie only after depression. She was on an emotional roller coaster ride, but thanks to Gwen things were getting better. Ruthie Mae had learned there are some things a person just cannot control. She was also now at the point of needing to find meaning for her suffering.

Tonight, Dr. Gwen Warren was giving her a way to find meaning. She was not certain what it was all about. Gwen had called earlier and asked if she could come over to Ruthie Mae's for a visit. Gwen said she wanted her to make a telephone call. She did not have to talk to anybody—just leave a message on an answering machine. Doing so would help find the murderer of Mildred Monroe, Gwen told her. Ruthie Mae did not need much convincing.

Gwen Warren dialed the telephone number and held the phone to her ear. After about twenty seconds, she held the mouthpiece about two inches in front of Ruthie Mae's mouth. The social worker nodded, and Ruthie Mae read.

"Mr. Boulder, please call Mary Copiah at two-oh-five-five-five-five-two-two-one-two. It is in regard to Mildred Monroe. Ask Ms. Copiah to tell you about Rico's mother and father."

Gwen took the receiver and replaced it on the telephone. Ruthie Mae looked at her counselor and asked, "Did I do okay?"

"You did fine," said Gwen Warren. "Just fine."

CHAPTER 29

Boulder left the Secretary of State's Office, picked up a bottle of Laura's favorite wine and headed home to prepare dinner. They both loved dining on his balcony overlooking downtown Jackson, but a cold front made it too nippy to be outdoors for a long period of time. The forecast low for tonight was thirty-eight degrees with winds gusting from fifteen to twenty miles per hour.

Once inside his home, Boulder laid out the ingredients for the spaghetti dinner and started boiling water in a stockpot. When the water was bubbling, he dumped pasta into the pot. Tonight he needed food, some wine and a good shoulder to cry on. Still unsettled from the events of the day, he thought of Rosey Adams. Any community could use more like him.

Dinner was almost ready when Laura walked in the door at 6:30 p.m. Boulder greeted her with a kiss on the cheek. "You're early. That's terrific! How did your case come out?"

"We won," she replied. "The jury stayed out less than an hour. A victory for trial lawyers."

"I thought you didn't like trial lawyers."

"I love trial lawyers. It is plaintiff lawyers I have the problem with. Somehow semantics is taking over the legal marketplace. Plaintiff lawyers are lawyers who sue. They represent people who are complaining about something. Trial lawyers are lawyers specializing in being in court and actually trying cases. Trial lawyers represent plaintiffs and defendants. I represent businesses when they sue or get sued. So that makes me a corporate trial lawyer."

"One of the good guys," he said.

"Don't get me wrong. The system needs plaintiff lawyers. In the old days, a poor person who had been victimized by a big corporation was unable to get justice. The poor person would go to lawyers only to learn that no matter how good the case, they would not be represented if they could not pay a retainer. Then came contingency cases. The poor person went to a lawyer, and, if he had a good case, the lawyer would take it in the hopes of winning and being awarded attorneys fees or getting a percentage of the award. Then, somehow, things got out of kilter—like when juries started making outrageous awards—and some greedy lawyers saw a way to get rich quick. But they needed clients who had been damaged, so they started advertising and things got crazy. Turn on the television now and you get bombarded with attorneys who want your business if you have been hurt in an accident. Let someone hurt in accident go to an attorney and it be discovered the defendant has no insurance. Good-bye victim."

"Sounds like you're getting cynical."

"I love my job. I'm just getting disappointed with my profession."

They moved to the table, and Boulder dimmed the lights and lit a candle. Although both of them loved dining out, they cherished dinners like this. They raised their wine glasses. One of their rituals was to trade turns making the toast.

"I believe tonight is your toast," Laura said, her glass held up.

"This is for Roosevelt Adams, the Chief Deputy of the Holmes County Sheriff's Office who died today of an apparent heart attack." Boulder's voice quivered as he continued, "A good man. I wish I had known him longer."

"Oh, Jack," Laura said. "I'm so sorry." She placed a hand on his. Each took a sip of wine. "Do you want to talk about it?"

"Not much else to say," Jack said, staring at his plate.

After letting the silence stretch between them, Laura finally broke his reverie by asking, "Have they recovered your car yet?"

"Oh," he said, coming back to life. "I haven't talked to you in two days." He told her about being on the Square in Lexington, seeing his car and then the car chase. "I'm thinking about driving it in the parade in Lexington on Saturday. They have an antique car parade every year. I think it's going to be part of the Christmas parade this year."

"What about your letters from the Lexington case?" she asked. "Did you get a chance to meet with Linda Youngblood?"

"She was very helpful. I'm learning a lot about churches."

"What do you mean?"

"Apparently—and I defer to your legal knowledge—you and I could form our own church. We could become a nonprofit organization and get a tax exemption and everything. Pretty strange to me."

"You're probably right," Laura said. "It's an unsettled area in the law in many ways. I'm afraid it has the potential to be the next big thing in the legal world."

"Why is that? Churches have been around ever since the country was founded."

"That's true," she said. "But churches are changing drastically every day. It used to be churches belonged to an established denomination. Nowadays, non-denominational churches are growing faster than mainstream denominations. There is no requirement that churches get a business privilege license, so yes, it is probably legally possible for you and I to start a new church, assuming it was not started as a sham and is really legitimate. Churches have splits in their congregations, and new churches start all the time. Where things will become confusing is when new non-Christian churches start outnumbering Christian churches. I would look for a lot of new litigation about how we define the term 'church' in our society."

"I had an interesting experience in a church yesterday." He told her about his interview with Reverend Robert Lauderdale. She picked up on the personal religious aspect of it.

"So, Jack. Are you saved?"

"Not you too?" he moaned.

"I'm not really serious, but it is something to think about. People should be able to articulate what they believe."

"Well, you had better believe a certain way or else someone in Lexington will try to save you."

He then told her about the case from start to finish. He said he believes one of the people on the list sent the letters, but he was not sure who or why. Was this a case of process of elimination or was there more to it?

"Do you think the murder of Mildred Monroe has anything to do with the letters?"

"I did not think so until I found her calendar and talked to Jerry Jasper at the Chicago P.D. There could be a link, but I'm not sure."

After dinner, each felt talked out. Both had two days of intensity behind them. At 7:45 p.m., Laura announced she needed to go home to prepare for a settlement negotiation first thing in the morning. They kissed good-night, again on the cheeks. As she was leaving, he wondered if the romance was fading. Probably so. They had been dating several years now. Last year he had asked her to marry him, but she said she wanted to keep the relationship the way it was. Her rejection had hurt his male ego, but he had gotten over it. She was his best friend and more. That was something a lot of married couples could not say.

A blinking red dot caught his eye. It was the answering system.

CHAPTER 30

Boulder dialed the telephone number. There was an answer at the second ring.

"Hello," came the monotone voice of a female who sounded as if she could be in the age range of over forty and under ninety.

"This is Jack Boulder. Someone left word for me to call this number in regard to Rico."

"What's he done?" The "what" came out as a "Whaas." He could almost smell the alcohol at the other end of the line.

"He's in jail in Mississippi," Boulder said.

She had received many such calls in the short period of time Rico had lived with her. She took him in when all the other relatives gave up on him. She believed she could make a difference. She found out quickly an incorrigible teenager and an old woman are no match. Most of the calls were from police departments in the Birmingham, Alabama metro area. For a kid who had no car, he was very mobile. Most of the time he was being charged with stealing or fighting.

"What did he do?"

"He is charged with murder."

"Why are you calling me?"

"Someone told me to call you and ask you about his mother and father."

"His mother gave up on him a long time ago. He ain't got no father."

Boulder grinned. He knew what she meant, but the way she said it sounded comical. He knew better than to laugh. This sounded like a woman who had done all she could do.

"Did his father leave when he was young?"

"Left before he was young."

"Where is his mother?"

"She's in jail too. Atlanta this time."

Boulder wondered what Ruthie Mae Hinds wanted him to find out about Rico's mother and father. From the sound of this phone call, there was not much to find out. Boulder knew better, but decided to ask anyway. "Where's his father?"

"Working."

"Working where?"

"What's it worth to you?"

"Maybe twenty dollars."

"It's worth a thousand times that much, but I'll tell you for ten times that much." The slur was still there, but not quite as bad.

"That would be two hundred dollars?"

"That's right," she said, extending the two syllables into four.

"How do I know you would be telling me the truth?"

"You don't." Darn. She was a good negotiator even if she was inebriated.

"How do we complete this transaction?"

"That's up to you," she said.

"What if I sent you a hundred dollars right now?"

"How you gonna do that?"

"I can do it on the Internet," Boulder said. "Send money from my account to yours electronically."

"I don't have no Internet."

"Do you have a computer?"

"Nope."

"I can send it by telegram," Boulder said. "Would that work for you?"

"Nope."

"Why not?"

"Because I only do business face-to-face," she said.

"May I call you right back?"

"It's your dime."

Boulder checked his caller ID and retrieved Ruthie Mae Hinds' telephone number. He dialed her number. She answered on the first ring.

"Ms. Hinds," he said, "This is Jack Boulder. You left a message for me to call a telephone number about Rico. I called that number like you said, but the person said she would not give me the information I requested unless I paid for it. She also said I had to come to Birmingham to get it. Is it worth it for me to go to Birmingham?"

There was a long pause. "What is your number? I'll call you right back."

He gave her his number. His telephone rang four minutes later. It was Ruthie Mae.

"Yes, Mr. Boulder. It is worth it for you to go to Birmingham. She's Rico's grandmother."

He called Birmingham back. The same voice answered.

"When do you want to do business, Ms. Copiah?" Boulder asked.

"I'll be up late, mister."

"What's your address? I'm on the way."

She gave him an address on Tuscaloosa Avenue in the western part of the city. Boulder used the Internet to find the location. He calculated it would take him three and a half hours to drive to Birmingham. Was this a wild goose chase?

CHAPTER 31

The night was clear and cold with a high canopy of glittering stars. Boulder headed east on Interstate 20. It was a straight shot from Jackson to Birmingham. He stopped at a truck stop the first ten miles of his trip and filled up on gasoline for his car and hot coffee for him. Then he did the math. Three and half hours there and the same amount back. It was now 8:10 p.m. Seven hours later would be very early in the morning indeed.

Fortunately, he got behind an eighteen-wheeler roaring down the road at a constant eighty miles per hour. Boulder settled in about fifty yards behind him. He arrived in Birmingham at 11:30 p.m. He found his exit and turned south toward Tuscaloosa Street, an area that had seen better days. He drove straight to the home of Rico's grandmother. The streets were quiet, owing to the cold weather and it being the middle of the week. During the summer, at this time of night, in this part of town, it was not unusual to hear gunshots.

Her house was a duplex in a block of duplexes. An old Buick passed by, wintry-white vapor swirling from its exhaust. The small front stoop was dark, but there was a light on inside. The curtain on the front window looked like a yellow, flowery, cotton sheet. Boulder parked across the street and walked to the front door, adjusting the ankle holster and the .38 Smith and Wesson Chief's Special. If this was a setup, at least he would go out with gun blazing. He rapped several times on the front door. From inside, he heard shuffling noises, and then she opened the door.

She was a big, stout woman with deep-set eyes that had bags under each one and were lined with crow's feet. She wore a huge blue, cotton housecoat. There was a recliner behind her with a reading lamp beside it. Across the room directly in front of the recliner was a large, flat-screen television. The house was neat and clean. Boulder did not smell any alcohol.

"What took you so long?"

"Traffic," he replied.

"We can save the conversation. I know what you came for and here it is." She pulled an envelope from her housecoat pocket and handed it to him. "I knew somebody like you would be here sooner of later. Funny thing is, I thought this would be different.

"What's in that envelope will help Rico. At least I hope it will. The boy was abandoned by his father. My daughter didn't know how to raise children. I could spank her for getting knocked up. She knew better. Come to think of it, I did spank her. She would have had a chance if she hadn't got pregnant." Boulder listened patiently as she went on. "Only thing I can do now is make sure the man that got her pregnant gets spanked a little, even if is too late to do any good. I just have one favor to ask you."

"What's that?"

"Use what's in the envelope to help Rico. He don't deserve it. He's a mean kid. But he never had a chance."

Boulder's curiosity was getting the best of him now. "Can I open the envelope now?"

"Why don't you just wait until you get in the car?"

Boulder reached into his jacket pocket and also pulled out an envelope. "Here's your money. I hope I got what I paid for."

"I can guarantee you right now you got more than what you paid for."

"And just how can you do that?"

She handed the envelope with the cash back to him. "You don't owe me a thing."

"Now I'm really wondering what's in this envelope."

"Mr. Curiosity Killed the Cat," she said and laughed. "You open that envelope when you get in your car. You called me to get information on Rico's mother and father. What you want is in there. But I'm telling you something right now. I'm not going to answer any of your questions, and I'm not going to open that door again when I close it behind you." She raised a finger. "Now hold on for just one minute." She turned and walked toward the kitchen, the floors creaking with each of her steps. "I'll be right back."

She returned and handed Boulder a plastic grocery bag filled with something. He opened it, looked inside and saw some chocolate candies, a bag of potato chips and a can of cold soda.

"What's this?"

"Something for the road. I would have put some hot coffee in there, but I don't drink the stuff."

"Thank you, Ms. Copiah."

Boulder turned and walked out the front door. Ms. Copiah shut it behind him. He walked across the street to his car and opened the envelope. The interior light illuminated the inside of the car. Inside was a certified copy of a Mississippi birth certificate. It showed the date of birth to be approximately seventeen and half years ago. The place of birth was Grenada, Mississippi. The name of the newborn was listed as Richard Copiah, the mother was Joanna Copiah. In the space for the father's named was typed "Gregory Greene."

CHAPTER 32

Rico Copiah reached up and pushed the bill of his dark blue baseball cap a little more to the right so it faced approximately forty-five degrees to the side. Into his wide nostrils drifted the body odor from his underarm. All the guys he had met in the organization had body odor. He belonged. Belonging was something he had searched for almost all of his life of seventeen and a half years.

When he was in elementary school in Memphis, other kids teased him because he was a slow reader. His fourth grade teacher told his mother Rico did not belong in fourth grade; he should never have been passed from third grade. So he had to repeat the fourth grade and then fifth grade. By the time he was in eighth grade, he had been failed three times, had lived in New Orleans with an aunt and in Birmingham with a grandmother, and had been arrested six times.

This past August, on the first day of school in ninth grade, he walked away from his grandmother's rundown house with three dollars in his pocket, ambled to the nearest automobile dealership, scoped out the cars on the lot until he found a used, two-year-old Honda Accord with the keys in the ignition, got in and drove it to Jackson, Mississippi, where it ran out of gas in a bad part of town. Just as he was abandoning the car, two guys in a new, black Cadillac Escalade pulled up and began questioning him. One was big, over six feet, two hundred pounds, and wore all black with turquoise jewelry on his neck, wrist and fingers. The other was medium height and wore a Chicago Bulls jersey. Both were in their twenties.

Each walked the tough guy walk and held their heads to one side.

"Where you going, man?"

"No place," he answered.

"This your car?"

He did not answer. He watched warily as the bigger of his two inquisitors walked slowly around the Honda, inspecting it as if it were a live animal at a livestock auction. The partner watched in silence, cutting his eyes back and forth between Rico and the other man. Rico had felt fear many times, but this time it was different. There was no adventure in this. He stole a glance at the surrounding area, figuring out the best direction to escape in the hot, humid, August late afternoon. The big guy walked to the back of the Malibu. They had Rico hemmed in. Big guy bent down and snatched off the cardboard tag. He held up the tag to Rico and said with a sneer, "You a car dealer in Birmingham?" Rico shook his head from side to side. "Is this car for sale?" Rico did not answer. Big guy turned to his partner and said, "I wonder how much he wants for this piece of crap?" Partner gave a huh-huh-huh laugh. Big guy looked back at Rico and said, "Three hundred is a fair price, don't you think?" Rico remained still. The only part of him that had moved was his eyelids, which had opened wider. Big guy reached in his pocket, pulled out a wad of hundred dollar bills, peeled off three of them, stuffed the currency in Rico's front pocket, and said, "Nice doing business with you, you little car thief. Now cross the highway and start walking back to Alabama. You turn around and look back at us and you get run over. You understand?"

Rico did as he was told and three hours later sat at a restaurant counter eating six Krystals and a large order of fries. As the last little morsel of hamburger went down his esophagus, Rico saw the two dudes who had hassled him earlier walk in the door. They walked up and stood on either side of him.

They ordered him outside and into their Escalade where they interrogated him with questions about where he lived, where he was going and how much he knew about stealing vehicles. After twenty-five minutes, Rico had become a candidate to join the organization. He met their basic qualifications: He was homeless, he was fearless, and he knew how to steal cars. They would furnish housing in a large house in an older section of Jackson. There were several of them living there now, and he could have his own bedroom. There was an initiation, however, that all members of the organization must pass. Prospective members could choose one of two tests. He must be able to drive away with a vehicle from an automobile dealer's lot within twelve minutes of being dropped off there, or he must carjack a vehicle worth over $40,000 driven by a male. Rico chose the latter method, and later that night he put a gun to a well-dressed man's head in the parking lot of an upscale restaurant and drove away with his BMW.

Things went well for Rico for a change. He had a group who respected his skills as a carjacker. He had money. He had a roof over his head. And his new friends liked to party hearty. Yes, this was the best time of Rico's life. Things were going well indeed, until Halloween night in Lexington. An order had come in for a Mustang. Jimmy DeSoto had relatives in Lexington, he visited them often, and during one of his visits, he had seen just the Mustang they needed. The plan was for Rico and Jimmy to wait in the parking lot and carjack the Mustang. DeSoto would do the carjacking, and Rico would drive the other car. For some reason, DeSoto shot the driver—a little old lady—and then told Rico to drive the Mustang. Rico had been caught after a wild chase and was now charged with murder and carjacking. Bail had been denied as he waited in the Holmes-Humphreys County Detention Center. He had not heard from anybody in the organization. So much for belonging. It looked like bad times were back for him.

"Rico," shouted the jailer. "Somebody here to see you." The prisoner was led to the visitor room where he could talk to a member of the free world using a telephone. A thick, plate-glass window separated prisoner and visitor. Rico picked up the phone and studied the man across from him.

"Rico Copiah?" Boulder asked.

He nodded affirmatively without answering.

"Do you have a lawyer?"

He nodded again.

"Who?"

He spoke into the phone. "Gus Rankin is my attorney."

"Thanks," Boulder said. "I'll talk to him." Boulder got up to leave.

"Wait a minute," said Rico. "Who are you?"

"Jack Boulder. I'm a private investigator."

"Did my lawyer hire you?"

"Not for your case."

"You know I didn't kill that woman, don't you?"

"Now how would I know that?"

"Because it's the truth," Rico said. Was that a pleading tone in his voice?

"I'll tell you what the truth is," Boulder said firmly. "You were at the scene. Her blood was on your shoes. Are you going to say your brother did it? Well, I've got news for you. He's going to say you did it. The district attorney is going to figure out which one of you is the better storyteller. He will then make a deal for one of you to testify against the other. This is a capital murder case. One of you will die; the other will spend the rest of his life at the state penitentiary. Now that's the truth."

"Mister, it ain't what it seems."

"What is it then?"

"Talk to Reverend Lauderdale," Rico said. "He knows I'm saved now."

"I've already talked to Reverend Lauderdale. If you're saved, then Reverend Lauderdale is happy."

"Would you call Reverend Lauderdale and ask him to come see me?" Rico asked. "I need to tell him something."

"Sure," Boulder said. "By the way, how old are you?"

"Seventeen."

"Do your mother and father know you're in jail?"

"No."

"Where are your mother and father?"

"No idea."

"What's your mother's name?"

"Joanna Copiah."

"What's your father's name?"

He hung his head. "I don't know."

"Does your mother know?"

"No."

"It's been tough for you, hasn't it?"

"Been tough for everybody," Rico said.

Boulder got up to leave. Rico stayed seated. As Boulder turned to walk away, Rico said, "Don't forget. Reverend Lauderdale."

CHAPTER 33

Boulder's next stop was the home of Ruthie Mae Hinds. He had no appointment, and he wanted it that way. She opened the front door on the second ring of the doorbell.

"Ms. Hinds?"

"Yes."

"I'm Jack Boulder, the man you called about Rico's grandmother."

"Yes."

"May I come inside? It's kind of cold out here."

"There's nothing I can tell you."

"Oh yes there is. You can tell my why you called me."

"I'm sorry Mr. Boulder, but I have nothing to say."

"Ms. Hinds. You look like a nice woman. And a truthful woman. I want to ask another question." She stood still, not giving any indication whether she approved or disapproved of his asking. "You were with Miss Monroe that night. Did you see who shot her?"

"No. I had already left when that happened."

"Thank you for your time, mam." Boulder said.

"You're welcome," she said. "If you would like to talk to somebody, you might want to talk to Dr. Warren—Dr. Gwen Warren—she has helped me quite a lot."

"Why would I want to talk to her?"

"I was just thinking you might," she said, as she closed the door.

CHAPTER 34

Callie Lee had arrived in Lexington two years ago as an intern with the criminal justice program at the University of Southern Mississippi. She liked the town and her work with the Holmes County Sheriff's Department so much, she was delighted when the Sheriff offered her a job after graduation. She served as a dispatcher, an office manager and an all-around organizer of things and people. She was also someone whom law enforcement officers knew would keep a secret. Consequently, she was the one whom everyone confided in. She was likable and efficient. She knew how to deal with an irate citizen as well as an out-of-control prisoner. Callie had wanted to be a police officer, but a bad case of osteoporosis, plus fifty extra pounds of weight and the inability to run a mile in twelve minutes were among the things that kept her from that goal. So she was doing the next best thing. The dispatchers worked rotating shifts, and as fate would have it, she had been on duty the night Mildred Monroe was shot, but had not been on duty the morning Rosey Adams had his heart attack.

She recognized the man who walked in the front door of the sheriff's office. He had been here before, working on some case with Chief Deputy Adams. She greeted him and said, "I don't think we have been introduced. I'm Callie Lee."

"I'm Jack Boulder. Chief Adams and I had been working on a matter involving one of your prisoners. His name is Jimmy DeSoto. I was wondering what the procedure might be for me to request an interview with him. I know he does not have to talk to me if he doesn't want to, but I would like to ask him."

"I'm afraid that won't be possible, Mr. Boulder."

"Really. Was he moved to another facility?"

"No. He posted bond."

"What?" Boulder said. "Do you know who posted his bond?"

"Yes sir. It was Attorney Gus Rankin."

CHAPTER 35

Boulder went immediately to Gus Rankin's office. There were too many unanswered questions in this case and most of them had to do with Gus. Furthermore, Boulder had the distinct feeling Rankin was avoiding him. Boulder parked in front of Rankin's office and went inside. If Rankin was attempting to avoid the private investigator it was no longer possible, for when Boulder walked in the reception room Gus Rankin was standing beside the receptionist with a handful of papers.

"Hello, Jack," Rankin said. "I'm glad you dropped by. How's your case with Gregory Greene going?"

"I'm not sure," Boulder said. "Is there someplace we can talk?"

"Of course. Come back to my office." He turned to his receptionist and said, "Hold my calls."

Boulder followed him through a doorway to a tiny hallway with only two doors leading from it, one to Gus' office and the other to another office slightly smaller. The second office had a table in the center piled with papers. These were definitely cramped quarters. Gus motioned Boulder to one of two chairs in front of his desk, closed the door and then took a seat behind his desk. Boulder was blunt.

"What's going on Gus?"

"What do you mean?"

"You recommend me to Gregory Greene, who hires me to find out who sent him a letter." Boulder paused as though he expected Rankin to show some form of agreement.

"That is correct. I thought you would like a business referral."

"I love referrals. What I don't love is when clients AND REFERRERS withhold vital information. I think it was rather important that you did not tell me about the murder of Mildred Monroe or the fact that Greene had been a student of hers.

"You are correct and I apologize," Rankin said.

"I also understand you are the attorney of record for Rico Copiah. It would have been nice to know about that."

"Again, you are correct; and again, I apologize."

"And now, I go to the sheriff's office to interview Jimmy DeSoto, the driver of MY stolen car and who is a suspect in the murder of Mildred Monroe, and they tell me he is out on bail and you are the one who bailed him out."

"Once again..."

"I know... I am correct and you apologize. Now tell me what in the name of everything sacred is going on in this town."

"I'll be glad to," Rankin said. He mashed a button on his telephone and said, "Would you step in here a moment?" The receptionist appeared instantly. Why the drama? He directed instructions to his assistant. "I know this may be impossible, but call Reverend Lauderdale and Dr. Gwen Warren and ask if they could come to a meeting in an hour. Before you call them, call and ask if we could borrow the conference room in the Rayner Building." He turned to Boulder and said, "My office is a bit short on conference space, and my fellow attorneys in the Rayner Building are good enough to let me use a real conference room."

"Whatever you say," Boulder said.

"It will be worth your time. I promise you." Ten minutes later, the assistant came in and announced the meeting was set. "Okay, Jack. The four of us will be meeting on the north side of the Square in the Rayner Building in an hour. You can't miss it. Make yourself at home in the meantime."

"I need some fresh air," Boulder said. "I need some sunglasses, too. I think I'll also do some Christmas shopping on the Square." He got up and left.

After Boulder had departed, Rankin's assistant commented, "I hope Mr. Boulder is not too mad."

"I just hope we can pull this off and stay within the limits of the law," Rankin told her.

CHAPTER 36

Boulder walked out of Rankin's office and collided with a passerby carrying a large bag of small items. The items, he noticed as they scattered across the sidewalk, were an assortment of cards, brushes, pins and small signs. He bent down immediately, apologizing as he did so. She was an attractive lady about his age. She wore blue jeans and a black sweatshirt with "Buy Local Art" printed on the front in lime green letters.

"I'm really sorry," he said. "My mind was in another part of the world." He glanced at her bag, a book bag upon which was printed, "Holmes County Arts Council."

"Are you an artist?"

"I'm more like a wannabe artist," she said. "I like being around art, so I volunteer to help with exhibits in the new building." She tilted her head toward a building down the street. "We will be open this weekend. Be sure to come."

"I'm from out of town, so I can't say for sure if I'll make it. Tell me about the exhibit. Is it a theme or one artist, or what?

"It's kind of chilly out here," she said. "Want to peek inside the building?" She led him to the gallery and they stepped inside. "I think the title of this exhibit is something like 'Works from the South.' I would call it 'Southern Potpourri'."

"Anybody famous?"

"We will have some works by Saul Haymond. He's the most famous artist around here."

"Didn't I read something about him recently in the New York Times?"

"Could be," she said. "He's well-known in certain parts of the art world."

That much was an understatement. Saul Haymond, Sr. is a self-taught artist whose paintings hang in homes, businesses, and governmental buildings in the United States and from Australia to Europe to South Africa. He was born in Ebenezer, a small community near Lexington. Each painting is distinctive, each has a history and a story, and his technique and style are unique. Saul Haymond has been recognized by the Museum Atelier A/E of New York City and in school textbooks as a unique talent of the twentieth and twenty-first centuries. He has been acclaimed with multiple fellowships: the Mississippi Arts Commission in both 1993 and 1998; the Adolph & Esther Gottlieb Foundation of New York City in both 1994 and 1999; the Southern Federation of Atlanta in 1994; the Ludwig Vogelstein Foundation of Hancock, Maine in 1994; the Pollock-Krasner Foundation of New York City in 1995; and the prestigious John Simon Guggenheim Memorial Foundation of New York City in 1999. Each fellowship carries with it a cash award restricted to the purchase of art supplies and materials and also the recognition associated with the fellowship.

Haymond began his career at the age of six or seven by doodling. Because of his talent in working with his hands, he traveled to Lantz, Maryland in his late teens as a representative from Holmes County in the Job Corps. This provided him the opportunity to receive formal art lessons, but because of his talent, he was soon the instructor. In 1964, Haymond exhibited his artwork in the Rotunda of the Capitol in Washington, DC, at Hagerstown Museum in Hagerstown, Maryland, and at both St. Mary's College (women's) and St. Joseph's College (men's) in Baltimore, Maryland. During this period, he crossed paths with such people as President Lyndon Johnson, Sargent Shriver (President Kennedy's brother-in-law), and Morris Udall. Shriver and Udall each purchased Haymond's paintings.

Those who were instrumental in assisting Mr. Haymond with his career during this time were Anson Peckham, Warner Cheek, Jack Wheat, and Ed Like. Haymond credits Clarence B. Rice with teaching him to read. Rice was connected with Howard University and tutored Haymond for two years, becoming both a mentor and devoted friend. Haymond affectionately refers to him as "my blue-eyed friend." In 1969, Haymond returned to Holmes County.

Twenty years ago, Haymond's artwork took a decided change. He began painting each canvas black to filter out the light before adding color. Haymond says of his artwork, "My paintings reflect our history. It was hard for some of us, but it made us who we are today. Hard work doesn't hurt us; it teaches us to appreciate what we've got." Haymond paints from his heart—his memories, his dreams, his visions, the stories he's heard over the years from his relatives.

"I've got to get to a meeting, but I'll try to come back for the show," Boulder says as he heads for the door.

"Great," she said. "Lots of art will be in here. Here, take a brochure from the Arts Council."

THE ARTS

The Holmes County Arts Council (HCAC) was established in 2002 under the leadership of an interested group of local patrons. Lexington Main Street Association donated the c. 1905 Flowers Mercantile Store to HCAC, and the organization immediately began fund-raising efforts to acquire matching funds for a Mississippi Arts Commission grant of over $150,000 to renovate the structure. Phase I of the renovation has been completed, and work is well underway on Phase II. The Holmes County Arts Council holds an annual Arts Gala each February as its primary fund-raising event and has successfully raised approximately $200,000 thus far.

The Lexington area lays claim to many successful musicians, authors, artists, and artisans.

Musicians include:

- The Preservation Singers, which is made up of volunteer musicians from across the area;
- Ora Catherine Reed, accomplished vocalist and musician;
- B.B. King, who lived in Lexington when he was fifteen and continues to have family connections in the city;
- Jesse Robinson, who spent many hours with his grandparents in Lexington and is currently plans to assist Lexington in establishing an annual Blues Festival;
- Grammy Award nominee Bill Ginn, who was a keyboardist, composer, arranger, and conductor;
- Blues man Otis "Big Smokey" Smothers; and
- Lonnie Pitchford, renowned blues musician and skilled instrument maker.

Authors include:

- Billy Ellis (*Tithes of Blood*);
- Melany Neilson (*Even Mississippi*, which received the Lillian Smith Award, the Mississippi Authors Award, the Gustavas Myers Outstanding Book on Human Rights, and a nomination for the Pulitzer Prize; and *The Persia Cafe*, which was published in 2001 to wide praise.); and
- the late Jonathan Henderson Brooks (*The Resurrection and Other Poems Collection*).

Artists include:

- Saul Haymond,
- Jonnie Crelan,
- Dick Temple,
- Beth Yates,
- Bruce Hill,
- E.W. Hooker,

- Helen Lammons,
- Ruth Richmond, and
- Barbara Parrish.

Artisans include:

- Bubba Barton (Ole Bridge Pottery);
- Billy and Kitty Ellis (Indian Bluffs Pottery); and
- Robert Holleman (Robert Holleman Pottery).

Back outside, Boulder looked at his wristwatch and saw he had twenty minutes until the meeting started. One thing small towns have over big cities is time. Because big cities require so much travel time, people rush and forget that small towns, where one can be anywhere in just a few minutes, are considered slower-paced perhaps because of travel time.

Glare from a passing car window almost blinded him, causing him to remember he was going to purchase a pair of sunglasses. He recalled a drug store in a small shopping center on Depot Street, out near where Dr. Gwen Warren's office was located. He drove there and pulled up in front of Russell's Drugs, Gifts, & Collectibles. The unassuming storefront belied what was inside. Not only was there a rack of sunglasses, there were gifts, pottery, tableware, collectibles and of course a pharmacy. Boulder went to the counter to pay for his sunglasses.

"Is that going to be all for you today?" asked a pretty girl behind the counter.

"That will do it," Boulder said. "Drug stores in Lexington are severely misnamed. You have everything in here."

"That's what a lot of people say," she said, and handed him a brochure. "Here. You can buy most of the gifts and collectibles through the Internet. Our website address is on there."

He walked out the door and covered his eyes with new polarized sunglasses. It was time for the meeting.

CHAPTER 37

Standing prominently on the north side of the Square, the Rayner Building is a brick, three-story, commercial building with a flat roof and parapet capped by concrete. Six rectangular recessed areas—smaller than normal sign-boards—adorn the parapet, above a heavy, pressed-metal cornice. "Rayner Bldg 1915" is spelled out above the third-floor windows. The first, second, and third stories are separated by concrete stringcourses stretching across the facade. The first floor features a three-bay storefront. There are two display areas of plate-glass flanking a central, recessed entrance of three glazed, wood doors. Storefront windows have wood sills and wood bulkheads. Three groups of tripartite, multi-light, leaded glass windows form the transom area and are delineated by two wood pilasters rising up from the storefront level. A flat, metal awning spans the facade, sheltering the first floor under the transom, which is supported on metal chains. A painted sign can still be seen on the west elevation in the upper wall, reading "Fincher Co. Hardware, Furniture." The word "Fincher" is spelled out in the tile leading to the recessed entrance. The building was completely refurbished in 2001 and houses Barrett Law Firm PLLC. The renovation, supervised by award-winning architect Belinda Stewart & Associates, received The Mississippi Heritage Award of Merit in 2002.

"Thank you for coming on such short notice," Rankin said. "I'll be as brief as possible. On October thirty-first Mildred Monroe was shot to death in a carjacking incident. There were no eyewitnesses, except those involved in the shooting. There was a police chase and an arrest. The person arrested that night was Rico Copiah, a seventeen-year-old. He refused to make any statements whatsoever and was identified by his wallet ID, which was later confirmed through his fingerprints. He's a rough kid with a bad background. The following day, November 1, Reverend Lauderdale here pays a visit to the jail, as he does rather often." Rankin looked at Lauderdale when he said it, and the pastor smiled with a nod of appreciation. "Rico and Reverend Lauderdale hit it off and..."

"I saved him," interjected the pastor.

"...Rico subsequently made a confession to Reverend Lauderdale. The confession had an extreme bearing on the case. Unfortunately, Rico let it be known he would not make any confessions to anyone else. Reverend Lauderdale contacted me and asked me what to do. I informed him there is a priest-penitent law in Mississippi deeming confessions to be privileged communication.

"Several days later, Rico began counseling sessions with Dr. Gwen Warren. He also made a confession to her. Again, there is a statute dealing with privileged communications as they relate to social workers and clients.

"Finally, Rico confessed to me about the events of that evening. As you know, there is also a communication privilege between attorney and client. Rico refused to make his confession to the sheriff's office or to put it in writing.

"In short, Rico gave each of us a confession, but none of us knew what he told the other. We were desperate to compare notes because what he told us was rather explosive. We talked to each other as professionals and realized we could not ethically disclose to each other what had been told to each by Rico.

We had long discussions about whether Rico was playing us against each other. The solution was right in front of me, but I did not realize it until one day when Gwen mentioned we would not be getting thank you letters this year from Mildred. I proposed Gwen hire me as her lawyer so she could confide in me, and the communication would be privileged. I then confessed to Reverend Lauderdale to be protected under the priest-penitent privilege. That way we could share knowledge about Rico's confession and compare notes. When we did so, we realized we also had to do something to draw out Gregory Greene. The thank you notes were the answer.

"Hold on a minute," Boulder said. "Are you going to tell ME what Rico said?"

"Sorry," Rankin said. "Privileged communication. But I think you will figure it out. Just bear with me."

"Sounds like you professionals over-complicated a simple matter," Boulder said. "You've been watching too much Boston Legal on television."

"Probably true," Rankin said.

"And do you think any of your privileged communications tactics will stand up in court?"

"Maybe not. But who's going to challenge it?"

"Okay," Boulder said. "Go ahead with the rest of it."

"Sending out the thank you notes worked," Rankin continued. "Gregory Greene called me. He was desperate to find out who sent the cards because he knew then one of us was aware he had been involved in Mildred Monroe's murder."

"And how were you aware of that?" Boulder asked.

"Just bear with me," Rankin said. "Gwen, why don't you tell Jack how you knew Gregory Greene was involved."

"Wait a minute," Reverend Lauderdale said. "She can't tell this private investigator what Rico said. Privileged communication, remember?"

"Then how are we going to tell Mr. Boulder what Rico said?" Gwen asked to no one in particular.

"What if Mr. Boulder was a pastor?" Reverend Lauderdale said.

"What!? I'm no pastor."

"You could be if you wanted to be," Reverend Lauderdale said.

"And how, pray tell—pun intended—would that happen?" Boulder said.

"You could be my associate pastor."

"Reverend Lauderdale does have a point," Gus Rankin said. "Each individual church or religious denomination sets its own standards for its clergy."

"Mr. Boulder has been saved," Reverend Lauderdale said. "He told me so."

"Have all of you gone crazy?" Boulder said. "Just stop with the confidentiality stuff. I will assume Rico told you that Gregory Greene had something to do with Mildred Monroe's death, the three of you tried to figure out a way to prove it, and you are trying to find out exactly how he is involved."

The three of them smiled and nodded like bobblehead dolls.

"I think I can fill in the missing pieces, but now Mr. Lawyer, it is I who has a confidentiality problem. I was hired by Gregory Greene. Don't I have a fiduciary responsibility to him?"

"It depends on the terms of your employment agreement," Gus Rankin said. "But without getting into a legal lecture, I will say, if you find your client is involved in criminal activity, you have no privileged communication statute to deal with. Private eyes don't have a privileged communication law yet."

"And I doubt they ever will," Boulder said. "May I present my take on this case? I think I can put it all together for you."

All of them placed their elbows on the table and leaned forward. "Go ahead," Rankin said.

"First, am I correct in assuming the three of you sent the thank you letters to Gregory Greene and Barbara Calhoun?" Each nodded slowly, glancing at each other to make sure that all were nodding. "I also assume you sent one to Barbara Calhoun because she was not in on the game and there was a possibility Greene might contact her. If he contacted any of you, you could just lie and tell him you received a thank you note, thought it was strange, and threw it away."

"Your assumptions are correct," Gus Rankin said.

"By sending a letter to Barbara Calhoun, you aided me greatly by confirming something I had suspected about Mildred Monroe. Although she was a wonderful teacher and person on one hand, she would resort to anything to save Saints College. She attempted to extort money from Clarence Calhoun. What she did to Gregory Greene caused her death."

CHAPTER 38

"Mildred Monroe had an ace in the hole when it came to extracting money from Gregory Greene. She got at least twice as much from him as she did each of you and she wanted even more." He paused and raised a hand. "I'm sorry. She did not get any money out of you did she, Reverend Lauderdale?"

"No," Reverend Lauderdale said softly.

"She got an extra portion from Greene, contributed it to Amazing Grace Church, and then had the church make a contribution to Save Our Saints. I trust that you retained an administrative fee for your efforts, Reverend."

"I did no such thing," he said. "She made out a check to the church; I made out a check to the SOS thing in the same amount."

"Good," Boulder said. "I'm glad we clarified that."

The three glanced at each other again. Boulder continued.

"Dr. Gwendolyn Warren," he said, focusing on her. She raised her chin. "I appreciate your not disclosing Rico's confession. Very professional of you. However, don't you think you should have told me you knew Mildred was extorting money from Greene?"

"How would I know that?" she asked.

"She confided in you, didn't she? You even took her to Jackson to catch a plane to Chicago and then picked her up when she returned. Didn't she tell you who she was going to see in Chicago?" Gwen Warren sat still and said nothing. "I think she told you a lot Dr. Warren. I think that she even told you that Rico Copiah was the illegitimate son of Gregory Greene. But you knew that already. You were in Gregory's class at Saints College. The rumors were strong, I'm sure. And that is why you had Ruthie Mae Hinds called to tell me to call Rico's grandmother. You knew she had the birth certificate, didn't you?"

"You are correct on all counts, Mr. Boulder," she said.

"So Mildred Monroe was extorting money, or blackmailing, whichever way you care to look at it, someone who had a lot of money and some vulnerability if it got out that he had neglected his fatherly duties. Just out of curiosity, what did Mildred say when she came back from Chicago? What did you talk about in the car on the ride back to Lexington?"

"She was pretty happy," Gwen Warren said. "She said the trip had been worth it and she now had enough to show the church that Saints College should be reopened."

"Although all of you, including Mildred, were probably using questionable methods for the greater good, there was something you did not know about Gregory Greene." He paused for effect and then continued. "He was a ruthless participant in an organized crime ring. And it was that ruthlessness that led him to order that Mildred Monroe be killed. The order went directly to Jimmy DeSoto, the Jackson leader of a nationwide car-theft ring. DeSoto needed a driver if he was to make it look like a carjacking. Rico just happened to be handy."

"He was a member of their organization," Gwen Warren said. "It was his only family."

They leaned back and exhaled. "Well, I'll be damned," Gus Rankin said.

Boulder looked hard at Gus and said firmly, "Now Gus, tell us why you posted bail for Jimmy DeSoto."

"I never would have done it if I had known about what you just said. I swear I wouldn't."

"It appears to me—and I would be interested if any of you know any differently—that it was coincidence that Rico was the driver," Boulder said. "I found no evidence to suggest that Greene even kept up with his son or the mother."

"What happens next?" Gwen Warren asked.

"It remains to be seen. The authorities in Chicago are onto Greene. It's only a matter of time until they get him. And I have a feeling it will be sooner than later."

CHAPTER 39

Conley Smith placed his fishing rod and tackle box on a large rock in the sand on the side of the river. He reached down into a brown paper bag and felt the cold package of medium-sized headless shrimp. It had been frozen when he bought it three hours ago, but with the exception of the center portion, it had now thawed. He took a pocketknife from his tackle box and cut open the package. Catfish loved shrimp. And he loved catfish. Ever since he was a little boy up until his current age of sixty-eight, he loved catching catfish from the river and taking them home to cook himself. He led a simple life and lived all of his adult life alone. A few years ago he retired from his job as a maintenance foreman for the County of Holmes. He now spent his days puttering around in the garden out back of his small two-bedroom house on the north side of town. His nephew, a real estate agent, told him he ought to consider selling and moving to a senior-citizen development. He told his nephew to give his real estate advice to someone who needed it. He was content to tinker around during the day and fish at night. He knew that there were catfish weighing over thirty pounds in this part of the river. It was his dream to catch a catfish weighing over twenty pounds before he died. He had a feeling this was going to be the year his dream came true.

He separated one of the shrimp from the glob and baited his hook with it. On the line approximately ten inches up from the bait was a nine-ounce lead weight. This configuration was used in river fishing to make the weight stay on the bottom while the bait fluttered above in the current. Catfish were bottom feeders and found this irresistible. Because catfish were known as scavengers, many people did not like to eat them. This perception had changed dramatically with the advent of pond-raised catfish, which were grown commercially in catfish farms in the Mississippi Delta. Smith did not care, however, to go to a store and buy filleted catfish. Catching them himself somehow made them taste better. He threw his line to the middle of the river and felt the current take the bait downstream at the same time the weight was taking it to the bottom of the river. The line drew tight and he waited for a bite. Two minutes later, a four-pound blue channel catfish had taken the bait and was reeled in by the fisherman. He knew it would be a good night for catfishing.

Two hours and twelve catfish later, he started walking the one hundred yards back upriver to his pickup truck, which was parked in a gravel area by the boat ramp. There was a quarter moon out tonight and he watched his step, looking down at the ground immediately in front of him more so than up at the horizon. The sandy riverbank contained waist-high bushes. When he reached the boat ramp, he turned up into the parking area where his pickup truck was parked. He did not look forward to skinning the catfish when he got home. Catfish had to be skinned, not cleaned like fish with scales. The best way to skin a catfish was to place it belly down on a board and drive a nail through its head into the wood, slit the skin just behind the gills, and then peel off the skin with pliers.

He noticed the black Mercedes parked across the way from his pickup. It was backed in, its bumper nudging the bushes. It looked brand new and expensive. He was careful not to shine his flashlight in the direction of the car. He knew from past experience that it was probably occupied by two young lovers who had found a great parking spot for necking and petting.

As he threw his stringer of fish into the back of his pickup, he noticed that the car was awfully still and quiet. Usually there would be some kind of movement or foggy windows if the car was occupied. Maybe there's another fisherman—a rich fisherman—on the river tonight.

CHAPTER 40

The telephone awakened Jack Boulder at 6:00 a.m. He let the answering machine take it. He would listen and then decide if he wanted to take the call. If it was like most calls at 6:00 a.m., it would be a wrong number and there would be a click from the answering machine after the caller realized the wrong number had been dialed. Such was not the case this time.

"Good morning, Jack. This is Jerry Jasper in Chicago..."

Boulder rushed the answering machine and picked up the receiver before Jasper could finish.

"Jerry," he said. "I'm here."

"Good. I have breaking news from Chicago for you. Our friend Mister Gregory Greene has ordered himself a new car. He's picking it up tonight in Mississippi. Thought you might like to tag along."

"Are you coming to Mississippi?"

"I'm on the way now in an FBI jet. Meet me at the Department of Public Safety headquarters in Jackson at one o'clock. Ask for Lieutenant Colonel Harrison with the Mississippi Bureau of Investigation. I'll fill you in when I see you."

"Ten-four."

Lieutenant Colonel Julian Harrison, Director of the Mississippi Bureau of Investigation, also known as the MBI, stood before a room of over twenty law enforcement officers representing federal, state and local agencies. The MBI has general police powers in Mississippi. Part of its responsibilities is to coordinate activities between federal, state, and local authorities involved in crime prevention and criminal investigations. As such, it has the responsibility through the Criminal Information Center for coordinating, sharing, and exchanging information with other agencies on an intrastate level concerning intelligence and other criminal activities. The upcoming operation exemplified the heart of the MBI mission.

"Welcome to Mississippi, Ladies and Gentlemen," said the director. "At this time, I would like to introduce the head of the combined interstate vehicle theft task force—Special Agent Fred Lowndes."

Lowndes moved to the podium at the front of the room and began speaking. "We have good intelligence that the coordinator of this network of car-theft rings is going to be in Mississippi picking up a new car that he loves. It's a Mercedes CL600, one of the finest automobiles made. It retails for over a hundred thousand dollars. I checked and found three of them for sale on dealers' showrooms in Chicagoland yesterday. However, our subject, Gregory Greene, would rather steal his than pay for it, even though he could easily afford it. The vehicle was taken from a shipment that he believes is running behind schedule, so he thinks he has plenty of time for a leisurely drive back to Chicago. Our latest statistical information is that Greene is responsible, directly or indirectly, for over five hundred vehicle thefts in the past three months, some of which have turned up in Iran. You may assume Greene will be accompanied by several subjects who will be armed. Our information is that the car is being driven to the pickup point as we speak. I'll now turn the meeting back over to Colonel Harrison for final details."

The meeting went on for another half-hour. Jack Boulder had been allowed in at the request of Lieutenant Jerry Jasper of the Chicago Police Department. Boulder had also been authorized to accompany Jasper as an observer.

CHAPTER 41

Fog rose from the river as the end of daylight approached and dusk took over. The day had been sunny, warming up the surface of the water. With the setting sun, the air was getting colder. The low tonight would be in the upper thirties, according to the weather report. The effect on the river was surreal. Conley Smith, the retired maintenance foreman and fisher of catfish, parked his truck in the usual place near the boat ramp and started walking toward the river. He noticed the Mercedes was still there from the night before. If it was still there when he came back later tonight, he might just call the sheriff.

He decided to try something different than his traditional fishing rig. Tonight he would rig a trotline and use it to catch ole Whiskers, the thirty-pound catfish he knew lay resting on the bottom of the dark river in the cold flowing current of the river channel.

Trotlines were long heavy lines that were rigged with shorter lines and extended out into the river from the bank. This type of rig presented a number of baits to the fish. Usually, a trotline fisherman would tie one end of the line to an overhanging tree limb, and place a fairly large weight—at least ten pounds—on the other end. The end with the weight would then be dropped in the middle of the river. Every ten feet or so along the trotline there would be normal fish lines of two to four feet in length with baited hooks on the end. Thus, a trotline of fifty feet could present five or six baits to the catfish. Every three or four hours during the night, the fisherman would harvest the trotline. A fisherman who set up five or six trotlines could have a very plentiful catch. A person like Conley Smith earned extra income selling such catches to local markets.

This time, the old fisherman was using a special, thin trotline made of metal wire. It was long enough to extend the entire 110-foot width of the river. His boat had a twenty-five horse-power outboard motor, but he did not need it while setting the lines. He tied his special trotline around a small tree on the bank of the river, then paddled across the still water in his small, aluminum boat and tied the other end of the line to a similarly-sized tree on the other side. This method allowed him to set up the baits while the entire line was out of the water. It was a much more efficient method than pulling up one bait line at a time. He did not have to stop and take off fish while baiting hooks. The trotline itself was approximately four feet above the surface of the water, something that was highly illegal because of the danger it caused for boaters on a river. But Smith knew that there would be no boaters on this river. After all, it was 5:00 p.m. on the second Saturday in December. After setting the trotlines, he pulled his boat up on the bank far enough to keep it from drifting away. He walked a quarter mile south and sat down on the bank. The stars would be pretty tonight.

At the parking area of the boat ramp, members of the inter-state task force were in place, hiding behind bushes and trees and far enough away that they could not be seen if someone in the parking lot were looking directly at them. The SWAT team members were wearing camouflage suits. The lighter side of twilight took the edge off the lines. Jack Boulder stood beside Lieutenant Jerry Jasper in the cold air, contemplating each exhalation of his breath.

At 5:10 p.m.. a white four-door Cadillac drove into the parking area. The still air amplified the tire noise on the gravel.

The Cadillac pulled up beside the new Mercedes CL600, and the driver shut off the engine. The night became quiet. The soft sounds of the gurgling water in the river wafted through the air. All four doors of the Cadillac opened at the same time; one man got out of each door. The four of them surrounded the Mercedes. Boulder instantly recognized the two men who emerged from the back doors. Gregory Greene and Jimmy DeSoto gave each other a high-five. It was his client and the thief who had stolen his Camaro.

"What do you think of it, my man?" Jimmy DeSoto asked.

"Just what the doctor ordered," said Greene. "Where are the keys?"

DeSoto reached in his pocket and tossed the keys to Greene. He stepped back and took one more admiring look at the $100,000-plus car, and then opened the driver's door. As he did so, Greene thought he saw something in the woods. Suddenly shadowy figures in camouflage suits appeared and surrounded him and his friends. One of them flashed a badge and exclaimed, "FBI. Don't move! You're under arrest for interstate transportation of a stolen motor vehicle."

Four sets of hands went up in the air. Other hands immediately searched the four of them. Guns were taken from all but the television weatherman from Chicago. Greene looked around and surveyed the situation. He studied the faces of the men who came in with him one by one. Before today, he had seen only one of them. His wrath turned to Jimmy DeSoto.

"You did this, didn't you? You're a dead man, you hear me. A dead man!"

"What are talking about?" DeSoto shouted.

"You set me up. That's what. When did you make the deal? When you were up in the jail in Lexington?"

"You're wrong! I don't know what you're talking about!"

Boulder stepped forward.

"What are YOU doing here?" Greene asked.

"Making sure you get your money's worth," Boulder said.

"What?"

"You hired me to find out who sent the letters from Lexington to you. So I'm going to tell you now." He paused. Greene stood staring at him. Waiting. "It was Mildred Monroe who sent the letters. She just used some others to send them for her."

"What are you talking about?"

"She tried to blackmail you, didn't she? Did she show you the birth certificate or just tell you your son might be looking for his daddy?"

"That woman was crazy. She never liked me anyway. She just used me to get all the other students to mind her."

"So you had her killed?"

"You can't prove that," Greene said.

"Oh, I think we can. Our star witness is right here," Boulder said nodding his head toward DeSoto. "How much did he pay you, Jimmy?"

"You can't prove a thing," DeSoto retorted.

"Well, let me explain how it works. It's like a little chain. Mr. Gregory Greene here is at the end of the chain. There is a link to him. That link is you. And you will testify he hired you to kill Mildred Monroe. The reason you will so testify is because Rico will testify he was with you when you did it and saw you do it. If that is not enough, we have the murder weapon, which was found in the car you were driving." Boulder grinned. "Do you see how it works now?"

They all stood quietly, considering this information. It was plainly dawning on them that their days in criminal entrepreneurship were about to end.

Greene suddenly bolted toward the river. One of the officers in camouflage raised his rifle.

"Don't shoot," commanded the Lieutenant. "I'll take care of him."

Greene reached the river and dove through the air. Not into the water, but into the fishing boat of Conley Smith. He landed belly-first inside the boat. The force of his landing pushed the boat off the bank and into the river. Greene was about to lose consciousness. The crash into the boat had probably cracked a rib. He felt immense pain from his rib cage and found it hard to breath. He looked and saw Lieutenant Jasper and Boulder running toward him. Somehow, he managed to turn around and find the electric starter that brought the outboard motor to life. He looked down at it, remembering enough from previous lake outings about how to put it into gear. He did so and twisted the handle. The little boat rose up and surged ahead into the fog. The boat quickly leveled out and Greene felt the moisture hitting his face. He looked back to see several law enforcement officers arrive at the river bank at the point from which he had just left. One officer dressed in black raised a rifle with a large scope, one that could gather light. Here in the shadowy dusk Greene knew that the officer had an easy shot. Greene prepared to die. He turned back toward the front of the boat and leaned forward as the propeller thrust the boat ahead. When the officer shot, it would hit him in the back. Someone would have to explain why a man was shot in the back. Even in death he would achieve the notoriety he had sought in life. The excitement was exhilarating. No, it was intoxicating.

But the officer did not fire. He just stood there. Why didn't he shoot? Of course. He could not shoot a man in the back. Greene realized that he would not to die after all. There would be more telecasts, more businesses to run, more worlds to conquer. Al Capone had nothing on him. Tomorrow he would prevail.

A big grin came upon his face. The grin then changed to a laugh. He had done it. He threw his head back and laughed heartily.

From his position downriver, Conley Smith heard the boat coming. Where did a boat come from? He was the only one on the river. Conley Smith got up and started running. He had to get to the trotline and get it down quickly or this fool would run into it. The boat was already almost too close to stop. He got to the trotline before the boat did and reached down in his tackle box for a pair of wire cutters to cut the trotline before the boat reached it. His heart was racing. With one hand on the trotline and one shaking hand in his tackle box, Conley Smith watched frantically as the speeding boat approached the thin wire that was stretched taut across the river. He could not comprehend the sight of a man dressed in a black trench coat, with head thrown up in laughter, speeding down the river in a boat. Smith had a flash of an image of a wolf baying at the moon at night. Was the man howling or laughing?

The howling weathercaster never saw Conley Smith or the wire that had been strung across the river. But Conley Smith saw the weathercaster when the wire severed his neck and decapitated his head from his body. It was a sight that Conley Smith would see every night for the rest of his life—his speeding fishing boat hurtling down the foggy river and a man in the back laughing at the moon at the time of his death.

CHAPTER 42

The official start time of the Christmas parade was noon. By 11:40 a.m., the crowd was already three-deep on every side of the Square, the best place to see the Lexington holiday procession of bands, floats, marching units, dance teams and other assorted entrants. The weather was a perfect blend of sunshine and cool air. It was a time when former Lexingtonians came back for homecomings and grandparents came to visit their grandchildren.

Bob and Margaret Simpson were in the latter category. Both had grown up in Holmes County, he in Tchula and she in Lexington. Now retired and living on the Emerald Coast in Florida, they returned to Lexington every Thanksgiving to the large house Margaret grew up in. They would arrive on Thanksgiving Eve and leave on the day after the Christmas parade. There was plenty of room in the two-story, six-bedroom home. Their children and grandchildren lived there now, just as Margaret's parents and grandparents had done. The house was a large, wooden, Gothic-Revival style with a wraparound front porch. Although they were high school sweethearts when Bob told her, "One day I'm going to ask the prettiest girl in Lexington to marry me," it was their sophomore year in college before she invited him to Thanksgiving dinner at "The Big House." His parents balked at the idea, feeling children should be at home with family on Thanksgiving. Bob pointed out that the families lived only eleven miles apart and, if necessary, he would eat twice or time it so he could have turkey and dressing at one family's house and pecan pie at the other. And then there was Christmas.

"You know what I really miss about the Christmas season in Lexington?" Margaret said.

"What's that?"

"Remember when the singers from Saints Academy would come by the house and sing Christmas carols in the front yard?"

"Oh, how I remember."

"Dr. Mallory would load them up on that flatbed trailer and take them to different parts of town. They would sing a couple of religious carols and then a couple of holiday carols, always concluding with *We Wish You a Merry Christmas*. And then Daddy would walk out and put ten dollars in the bucket with the red ribbon around it. She really knew how to raise money."

"And remember the singing group—what was it?—yes, the Jubilee Harmonizers. She took them across the country raising money and acquiring books for Saints Academy."

"You know what I really like about the Christmas season?" Margaret said.

"What's that?" Bob replied, as he reached up and put his arm around her shoulder. They were standing in front of the *Holmes County Herald* on the east side of the Square, the same place they had stood for every Lexington Christmas parade in every year of their lives. Their children and grandchildren were across the street on the Courthouse lawn, allowing the little ones more space to frolic before the parade started.

"The people around this Square. Just look. All ages. All races. Everybody's happy. They are with their families. They say that Saturdays in Lexington was at one time the best time for the Square. I have to disagree. I'd say it's the Christmas parade."

"Hard to argue with that," he replied. "But I confess to liking the Square better at night during the Christmas season. It still amazes me to look up and see those strings of lights from the top of the clock tower stretching to the corners of the building. And all the lights on the buildings at night make it Christmas cozy to me."

"And sort of mysterious?" she said.

"There you go again. I'm the night person and you're the day person."

"Isn't that the way it is?"

"I suppose you're right. Hey, here comes the start of the parade."

A high school marching band led the parade. Four blocks behind them, the antique car section of the parade was about to move out. The cars were lined up in order of age, with the oldest cars being first. The leader of the car pack was a Model T that had been faithfully restored and driven about six times a year by a local car collector. He had three other cars in the parade—a 1932 Ford Coupe, a 1932 red Ford pickup, and a 1957 two-tone turquoise Chevy.

Jack Boulder was the driver of the next to the last car in the line. Behind him was a 1969 green Dodge Super Bee that looked like it had just been driven off the showroom floor. As the cars in front of him moved out, he reached down to the chrome gearshift knob, pushed it into first gear and let up on the clutch. The 1968 Camaro inched forward. Boulder smiled and turned to his passenger, Laura Webster.

"This reminds me of high school," he said and moved his right hand to the top of her left thigh.

"It sure does," she said with a grin as she reached down and removed his hand. "Watch your driving."

They drove the parade route, smiling and waving at the parade watchers. When it was over, they headed west out Highway 12 for the sole purpose of merely driving around.

Between Lexington and Tchula, the forested hills of central Mississippi suddenly and dramatically change to flat terrain. It is among the richest agricultural land in the world. One can stand on the bluff and gaze westward and see no end to the flat land. On Highway 12, just before the bluff meets the Delta land is Rosebank-Mt. Olive Road, which Hubert Washington had told him was the most scenic drive in Holmes County. Boulder turned right on the little-known road, and he and Laura rode the crest of a high hill overlooking the Mississippi Delta, a place having immense influence on the history of Lexington.

CHAPTER 43

The funeral of Roosevelt Adams was held the following Monday. After an opening prayer, these are some of the words that were said. . .

By the pastor: *"There are those who share their faith from the pulpit, or the podium, or the radio microphone, or the television. There are those who let their faith be shown by the way that they act instead of the way that they talk. Rosey Adams was a man whose actions spoke loudly of his faith. When the church needed a new organ, a fund-raising drive was held. I was stricken to learn we came up thousands short of the goal. Rosey called me and said he would be interested in contributing the balance needed under one condition. And that condition was his donation be kept anonymous until he was no longer on this earth. Well, it's time you know."*

By the mayor: *"Rosey Adams could have lived anywhere. He chose to live in Lexington. Rosey Adams could have chosen not to work at all. He chose to work in service to the citizens of Lexington. Our community is grateful for Rosey Adams."*

By the governor: *"Holmes County has produced many famous and notable people. Among them are Edmund Noel, who served as governor; Robert Clark, who was the first African-American since*

Reconstruction to be elected to the Mississippi House of Representatives; Saul Haymond, who gives America great art; Hazel Brannon Smith, the first woman to win the Pulitzer Prize for editorial writing; and Charles Mason, founder of the Church of God in Christ. And then there was Roosevelt Adams, who gained national fame in the sports world, yet came back to the town he loved and that loved him. In that sense, I must confess a bias: I wish more Mississippians who gain national fame and wealth would come back to their hometowns."

By a professional football player: *"Thank you, Lexington, for an athlete who was filled with the character and leadership our team needed. He kept us in line. I don't know if anybody noticed it or not, in these days when what players do off the field makes as much news as what they do on the field, but our team had no off-the-field incidents resulting in disciplinary action while Rosey was there. The sports media thought it was the coach. Not so. It was Rosey. He kept us in line and was our conscience. When anybody got close to getting out of line, he would pull them back in. When we won our first division championship, but then lost the conference championship, the team was really down. It took us less than a week to get back up. How so? Within seven days Rosey had a dozen roses sent to every player with a note that said, "Thank you for helping us bloom this year."*

Afterwards, Reverend Robert Lauderdale sang a solo of all verses of Roosevelt Adams' favorite hymn, *Shall We Gather at the River.*

And the congregation said, "Amen."

APPENDIX

BankPlus
Peoples Drug Store
Russel's Drugs, Gifts, & Collectibles
Lexington Main Street Association

BankPlus

Founded in Belzoni in 1909 as Citizens Bank & Trust Company, BankPlus began with a single office. Everyone worked hard and discovered that when people get a little more than they're expecting, they become a loyal customer for life. A simple but profound idea that has guided us for nearly a century.

Commitment

In 1994, we changed our name to BankPlus. This was more than a simple name change. It was a re-dedication to offering superior products and service. To go with our new name, we created the slogan, "It's more than a name. It's a promise." A phrase that reflects our desire to offer enhanced services and emphasizes our commitment to giving our customers more for their money.

Since our name change, this dedication has helped BankPlus become one of the fastest-growing banks in the entire region. Nevertheless, however big we grow, we remain proud of our community banking roots and strive daily to maintain and build upon that dedication.

Holmes County

In 2000, that growth included banking offices in Lexington, Durant, Pickens and Tchula when BankPlus acquired First National Bank of Holmes County. Started in 1929 on the square in Lexington, First National Bank of Holmes County had a commitment to economic growth and community that remains a cornerstone of the BankPlus way of doing business.

It's All About Community

At BankPlus, we are passionate about supporting community causes with time as well as money. We also look forward to continuing our tradition of community service everywhere we call home. Whenever our friends and neighbors need a helping hand, the people of BankPlus will always be there for them.

Member FDIC

Peoples Drug Store
c. 1920 BEALL'S DRUG STORE

Peoples Drug Store is located in the c. 1920 former Beall's Drug Store building on Lexington's historic Court Square.

A two-story red brick building on a corner lot, it has a two-course band of tan brick, slightly projecting from the façade wall and forms a stringcourse above the second floor windows. The second floor has six bays, symmetrically spaced. A canvas awning spans the façade. The interior features the original pressed tin ceiling and cornice work.

In 1984, David Dillon purchased Peoples Drug Store. Daughter Dayle graduated from the University of Mississippi School of Pharmacy in 1995 and returned to Lexington in 1998.

In 2002, there was a complete interior renovation of the gift area of the store, with the addition of new core lines such as Vera Bradley, Gail Pittman Pottery, Southern Belle T-shirts, Casafina Dinnerware, Made in MS products, Bridgewater Candles, Wicks 'n More candles, Le Creuset, and a wide variety of baby and child gift items, many suitable for monogramming.

Peoples Drug Store participated in Celebration Village in Tupelo, MS in 2004 and in Mistletoe Marketplace in Jackson, MS, in 2006 with an invitation to return in 2007.

Awards: David Dillon received the 2003 Lexington Main Street Association (LMS) Booster of the Year, and Dayle Diffey received the 2006 LMS Spirit of Main Street Award and Mississippi Main Street Association 2007 Downtown Revitalization Merchant of the Year Award.

Peoples Drug Store
P.O. Box 510, Lexington, MS 39095
www.peoplesdrugstore.net, 662.834.2721

Russell's Drugs, Gifts, & Collectibles

Russell's Drugs, Gifts, & Collectibles opened its doors February 6, 1986, as a pharmacy. The gift department was added in the summer of 1987 and has grown exponentially.

The Russells annually attend market in Atlanta and/or New York City to seek the best selection of gifts and home accessories.

Just prior to the holiday season of 2000, a vast two-story expansion was unveiled, adding welcomed room for Russell's signature lines, such as Wedgewood, Spode, Waterford, Vietri, Mississippi products: Good Earth and Peter's Pottery, and a generous assortment of gourmet food items.

Russell's Drugs, Gifts, & Collectibles
334 Depot Street, Lexington, MS 39095
662-834-1154, www.russellsgiftstore.com

The Ellington House

The c. 1910 Ellington House is a two-story house with hipped roof of asphalt shingles and brick foundation. A central cross-gable pierces the roof at the façade. The second story has five bays. The first floor is sheltered by a full-width hipped-roof porch with a small, front-facing gable at the center, supported on un-fluted columns and two engaged columns on the façade wall. Under the porch are three bays and a central leaded glass wooden door with leaded-glass sidelights and transom flanked by two single, wide windows.

The house is located on Race Street, named because a blacksmith and livery stable were once located to the rear of the Ellington House; the street in front of the house became known for its horse racing.

In 1989, the home was completely restored by the present owners, Billy & Sheila Russell.

LEXINGTON

Lexington, Mississippi, located at the geographical center of Holmes County, was founded for the purpose of serving as the county seat, incorporated February 26, 1836, with a population of approximately four hundred, and named in honor of Lexington, Massachusetts.

Otha Beall and Samuel Long donated sixty acres for Lexington's incorporated area, carefully planned with parallel streets emanating from a central square. By 1905, the town's population had grown to 2,134 residents, and the town was officially designated to the status of a city.

As the county seat, Lexington continues to be the hub of county government. The original courthouse was a rustic log structure. Renowned architect William Nichols designed the second courthouse; it burned in 1893. The present courthouse, located in the center of Court Square, was designed by a Knoxville, Tennessee firm and erected in 1894 at a cost of $22,000.

During Reconstruction, it was proposed to combine Holmes County and adjacent Attala County, moving the county seat from Lexington to Durant, Mississippi. Black Holmes County Representative H. H. "Buck" Truhart successfully thwarted this effort.

Early schools in Lexington included The Lexington Male & Female Academy, incorporated in 1844, later changed to Central Mississippi Normal College in 1854. It was housed in a two-story brick structure designed by architect William Nichols who died in 1853 while working in Lexington and was interred at Odd Fellows Cemetery. Other early schools included The Lexington Male Academy established in 1859, and the Lexington Normal College established in 1889.

In 1918, Miss Pinkie Duncan began the Saints Home School for Negro Boys & Girls. Dr. Arenia Mallory moved to

Lexington in 1926, resulting in the establishment of Saints Junior College and Saints Academy, the first privately-owned black boarding school and junior college in the nation. Saints' Jubilee Harmonizers entertained President and Mrs. Franklin D. Roosevelt at the White House in 1938.

Holmes County is the birthplace of the 4-H Club movement. On February 23, 1907, William Hall "Corn Club" Smith invited interested Holmes County citizens and Professor Perkins of A & M College to an organizational meeting of the first Corn Club. In the fall of 1907, Dr. Seaman A. Knapp, USDA special agent to the Southern States to promote agriculture, appointed Smith collaborator of the USDA. The Holmes County Club became the first federally sponsored club in the United States, and Smith became the first federal agent for club work. The movement quickly spread throughout the nation under the name of 4-H Clubs, which asks youngsters to "Make the Best Better."

Robert George Clark, Jr. was born on October 3, 1928, in Ebenezer, Mississippi; he earned an undergraduate degree from Jackson State University, a master's degree from Michigan State University, and also studied at Mississippi Valley State University, Florida A & M University, Western Michigan University, and the John F. Kennedy School of Government at Harvard University as a 1979 teaching fellow. Clark was elected to the House of the Mississippi Legislature in 1968, becoming the first African-American elected to the Mississippi Legislature since Reconstruction. During his tenure of service, Clark demonstrated his character as a statesman, rising from freshman lawmaker to the Office of Speaker Pro Tempore of the House in 1992. Clark reared his two sons by his deceased wife Essie before his marriage to the former Jo Ann Ross. His younger son Bryant now serves Holmes County in the House of the Mississippi Legislature. Both Robert Clark III and Bryant Clark are successful attorneys in Lexington, Mississippi.

Phillip Watson (Phillip Watson Designs, Inc., Atlanta, Georgia) is a Lexington native and returns to his hometown each year to oversee the annual Garden Seminar hosted by the HCAC. With a BS in Horticulture from Mississippi State University, his specialty is pattern gardens (parterres, knots, mazes). Watson designs and installs gardens throughout the country; is currently garden host on QVC television electronic retailer where he promotes plants for Cottage Farms of Mobile, Alabama; has been featured in the *New York Times*, the *Times of London*, *Southern Accents*, *Horticulture*, *House and Garden*, *Veranda*, and *Southern Living*. His work has appeared in the film *The Stepford Wives* and the CBS reality show *Wickedly Perfect*. As a frequent lecturer all over the world, Watson has spoken at a wide range of American venues, as well as, The Rosemary Verey Symposium in London, England.

On April 26, 1996, Milton Lee Olive III was posthumously awarded the Congressional Medal of Honor for his ultimate sacrifice in Phu Cuong, Republic of Vietnam, October 22, 1965. His citation read, "For conspicuous gallantry and intrepidity at the risk of his life above and beyond the call of duty. Pfc. Olive was a member of the 3rd Platoon of Company B, as it moved through the jungle to find the Viet Cong operating in the area. Although the platoon was subjected to a heavy volume of enemy gunfire and pinned down temporarily, it retaliated by assaulting the Viet Cong positions, causing the enemy to flee. As the platoon pursued the insurgents, Pfc. Olive and four other soldiers were moving through the jungle together when a grenade was thrown into their midst. Pfc. Olive saw the grenade, and then saved the lives of his fellow soldiers at the sacrifice of his by grabbing the grenade in his hand and falling on it to absorb the blast with his body. Through his bravery, unhesitating actions, and complete disregard for his safety, he prevented additional loss of life or injury to the members of his platoon. Pfc. Olive's extraordinary heroism, at the risk of his life above and beyond the call of duty are in the highest traditions of the U.S. Army and reflect great credit upon himself and the Armed Forces of his country." Olive was born November 7, 1946 in the Ebenezer community and is buried in West Grove Missionary Baptist Cemetery near Lexington.

Community organizations include the Boy Scouts of America, Community Culture & Resource Center, Friends of the Lexington Public Library, the Girl Scouts of America, Holmes County Arts Council (HCAC), Holmes County Chamber of Commerce, Lexington Main Street Association (LMS), Lexington Rotary Club, the Magnolia Garden Club, The Masons, the Preservation Singers, the Red Hat Club, and Triad.

LMS was established in 2001 and has successfully completed several community improvement projects. Each fall LMS hosts TASTE BUDS Cooking Competition, its annual fund-raiser for the organization. This event includes a Celebrity Taster, "Tasting & Tipping," live musical entertainment, and a Silent Auction.

Lexington boasts over 225 contributing buildings on the National Register of Historic Places, with six sites listed as Mississippi Landmark structures: Holmes County Courthouse, Holmes County Jail, Chancery Clerk Building, Confederate Monument, Masonic Building on Court Square, and HCAC Complex.

Antebellum development in Lexington showed the relative prosperity of the first settlers. Still standing are many homes that date back to the mid-1800s. Lexington suffered little or no damage during the Civil War due to its lack of railroad and other transportation-related resources.

The c. 1850 Walker Brooke House is a clapboard structure with a central, front-gabled, two-story section flanked by two side-gabled, one-story wings. The central section's pedimented gable shelters a two-story, undercut porch. The second-floor porch features jig sawn brackets and boxed columns, slightly battered, topped by ornate jig sawn capitals resembling palm fronds and connected with punched and jig sawn balustrade. The present owners are Jane and Holt Smith, who both have Holmes County roots dating to the 1840s.

The c. 1870 Judge Drennan house is two-story, clapboard and drop-sided bayed house with Italianate and Colonial Revival details. The hipped and cross-gabled roof is sheathed in metal or asbestos cement shingles. The front-gable is to the right on the façade, featuring a raking cornice with returns and carved consoles, with a round-headed, 2/2 window in the gable end, a paired segmental-headed window with pedimented surround in the second story, and a bay window in the first story. The bay, decorated with carved brackets, is under a separate hip roof. The house has had few owners and was purchased by the current owner in 1985.

The c. 1920 Porter & Sons' Funeral Home is a one-and-a-half story, drop-sided bungalow with a hipped roof of asphalt shingles and a brick-pier foundation in-filled with brick. A small, gabled dormer pierces the center of the front slope and has two single-light windows. An undercut porch, originally full-width, now covers two-thirds of the west façade, with the other one-third having been enclosed. Sheltered under the porch are a glazed, wood door with one-light transom and a paired 1/1 double-hung window in a wood frame to the right. A brick chimney is on the interior, on the center ridge of the roof. The chimney is central to tripartite hearths, each with its original c. 1920's tile work and original mantels. The doorframes and casings are original to the house. Porter & Sons' Funeral Homes was established in 1979 by Mr. Lindbergh Porter, Sr. Instrumental in the renovation of the structure were Mr. Porter, his wife Bernice, and their children: Lindbergh Jr., Pat Noel, Byron C., and Bonita.

The business was incorporated in 1999, following the death of Porter Sr. and today is still run by his children.

The Flowers Home is listed on the National Register of Historic Places in Lexington, MS. It is a c. 1920 one-story brick Craftsman bungalow and was originally the home of the Flowers family, who owned the adjacent Flowers Mercantile Building. After being vacated by the Flowers family, it served for many years as the office of the Holmes County engineer, J.C. Patton. It was later converted for use as a local flower shop and recently has been renovated for use as the law offices of Clark & Clark, PLLC.

The c. 1885 (old) Bank of Commerce is the oldest commercial building in Lexington. It is a two-story, red-and-brown-brick commercial structure on a corner lot with a side-gabled roof of asbestos-cement or slate shingles. The façade parapet is shaped and features a steel capital. A concrete signboard is in the upper wall above the four bays of the second floor. A canvas awning shelters the transom and storefront areas and wraps around to the south elevation. Holmes County Farm Bureau currently occupies the building and completed a total interior and exterior restoration of the property at a cost of over $80,000 in 2006.

Architectural information from the U. S. Department of Interior, National Park Service, NATIONAL REGISTER OF HISTORIC PLACES, Lexington Historic District, Lexington, Holmes County, Mississippi, November 2000

Lexington Main Street Association
103 West China Street, Lexington, MS 39095
662-834-0053, www.lexingtonms.com.

The Mississippi Mysteries Series

The Mississippi Mysteries Series began as a community development project in the small Mississippi town of Flora, located in the central part of the state. The community was starting a chamber of commerce and wanted a unique way to promote the town. The incoming chamber president approached Phil Hardwick, a well-known columnist for the *Mississippi Business Journal* and instructor at Millsaps College, about the possibility of writing a book of fiction set in the small town.

Hardwick loved the idea of creating a fictional story set in real places. He planned to treat his readers to a good mystery with the goal of inspiring them to visit the places mentioned in the novella. In 1996, *Found in Flora* was published with a 500-copy printing and sold out immediately.

Other communities heard about the project and asked for books set in their towns. There are now 10 volumes in the series: *Found in Flora, Justice in Jackson, Captured in Canton, Newcomer in New Albany, Vengeance in Vicksburg, Collision in Columbia, Conspiracy in Corinth, Cover-Up in Columbus, Sixth Inning in Southaven,* and *Letters from Lexington.*

The Series features Jack Boulder, a private investigator based in Jackson who solves cases in towns around the Magnolia State. It is worth noting that all of the towns in the series are Main Street communities. Main Street is a program of the National Trust for Historic Preservation.

Hardwick is now concentrating on his Great American Mystery Series featuring Jack Boulder on the case in individual states across the country.

For more information, visit:
www.philhardwick.com
www.greatamericanmystery.com

The Great American Mystery Series

Phil Hardwick's Great American Mystery Series will be modeled after the Mississippi series in that each book will feature one or more communities in a state. As with the Mississippi series, readers will be treated to a mystery that is fictional yet set within real places. Recurring character Jack Boulder, a private investigator, will expand his territory to include the entire country.

Local community organizations, such as Main Street programs or chambers of commerce, will be engaged as sponsors of the books. It is author Phil Hardwick's goal to have a book set in every state. Hardwick will select states and communities based on their enthusiasm for the project and the uniqueness of the settings. So how does a community become the subject their state's book? A community representative should call Hardwick's publisher toll-free 1.866.625.9241. More information is available at www.philhardwick.com and www.greatamericanmystery.com.

Phil Hardwick

Phil Hardwick loves a good mystery. Early in his career, he solved real ones as a police officer and state investigator. These days he's a professional economic and community developer who spends his spare time writing mysteries. Phil is an award-winning columnist whose column, "From the Ground Up," appears bi-weekly in the *Mississippi Business Journal*.

He is Past-President of the Mississippi Main Street Association, Mississippi Economic Development Council and Mississippi Sports Hall of Fame and Museum. He received his undergraduate degree from Belhaven College and MBA from Millsaps College. He is a graduate of the Senior Executives in State & Local Government executive program at the John F. Kennedy School of Government at Harvard University. During his military service, Hardwick was Security Team Leader for Army One, the Presidential helicopter.

More Books Available from Great American Publishers

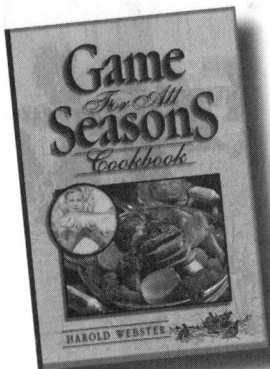

Game for All Seasons • $16.95 • 240 pp • 7 x 10 • paperbound • 292 seasonal recipes for 30 varieties of game presented in an easy-to-follow format plus fascinating stories about capturing, cleaning and cooking the game. The perfect gift for hunters and fishermen.

Tennessee Hometown Cookbook • $16.95 • 240 pp • 8 x 9 • paperbound • We're dishing up a double-helping of local, tried and true recipes and fun-filled facts about hometowns all-over the state. Tennessee brings to mind music and mountains, history and heritage, and good food – get a taste of it all in *Tennessee Hometown Cookbook*.

Visit is on the web...

www.GreatAmericanPublishers.com
...to win a free book, get terrific recipes, and more.

Call toll-free for more information:
1.866.625.9241

100% Satisfaction Guaranteed

One Foot in the Kitchen Cookbook Series
Each book: • $12.95 • 160 pp • 7 x 7.5 • paper

Quick Crockery Cooking—You'll be in and out of the kitchen fast with creative crockery recipes that are easy, economical and DELICIOUS.

Quick Desserts—Get out of the kitchen and into the fun with more than 150 recipes for the best-tasting desserts of all time.

Quick Hors d'oeuvres—Entertaining friends and family is a snap with quick and easy recipes for all-time favorite hors d'oeuvres and beverages.

Quick Lunches & Brunches—From Shrimp Scampi Kabobs to Caramel Muffins, impress friends and family with a delicious brunch made from 150 quick and easy recipes.

Quick Mexican Cooking—More than 150 quick and easy recipes for meal after meal of pure Mexican pleasure.

Quick Soups 'n Salads—Preparing delicious, nutritious soups and salads has never been easier.

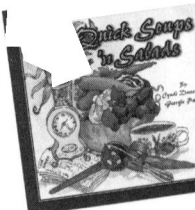